Pride & Pestilence

A Victorian Crime Thriller

Carol Hedges

Little G Books

Copyright © 2024 by Carol Hedges
Cover Artwork and Design by RoseWolf Design

All rights reserved.

No part of this book may be used or reproduced in any manner whatsoever without written permission of the author except for brief quotations used for promotion or in reviews. This is a work of fiction. Names, characters, and incidents are used fictitiously.

This edition by Little G Books (April 2024)

To Avalyn & Edward

About the Author

Carol Hedges is the successful British author of 20+ books for teenagers and adults. Her writing has received much critical acclaim, and her novel Jigsaw was shortlisted for the Angus Book Award and longlisted for the Carnegie Medal.

Carol was born in Hertfordshire, and after university, where she gained a BA (Hons.) in English Literature & Archaeology, she trained as a children's librarian. She worked for the London Borough of Camden for many years subsequently re-training as a secondary school teacher when her daughter was born.

The Victorian Detectives series
Diamonds & Dust
Honour & Obey
Death & Dominion
Rack & Ruin
Wonders & Wickedness
Fear & Phantoms
Intrigue & Infamy
Fame & Fortune
Desire & Deceit
Murder & Mischief

The Spy Girl series
The Dark Side of Midnight
Out of the Shadows
Dead Man Talking
Once upon a Crime
Ready Deadly Go

Acknowledgments

Many thanks to Gina Dickerson, of RoseWolf Design, for another superb cover, and to my editor. Also, thank you to all friends on social media who comment, encourage and inspire me to keep writing.

I also acknowledge my debt to all those amazing Victorian novelists for lighting the path through the fog with their genius. Unworthily, but optimistically, I follow in their footsteps.

Pride & Pestilence

A Victorian Crime Thriller

London, 1870. A late afternoon in an early summer, with a pale sun shining limply down from a watery sky. Business is ending for the day; small girls selling violets around St Paul's have packed up their baskets and departed, along with the watercress sellers. Sandwich-board men have laid down their heavy placards and ceased from pounding the pavements. The Italian hokey-pokey men have melted away. Clerks scurrying from Lincoln's Inn to the Courts are now scurrying in the opposite direction. Omnibuses, crammed with homeward-bound passengers, clop steadily along the rutted streets, their knifeboards full. All is hustle and bustle in the greatest city on earth.

Look more closely. Hurrying along the footway is a young labouring man in muddy corduroy trousers, mud-caked boots, and an out-at-the-elbows mud-stained tweed jacket. He has a flat cap above a dirt-encrusted and unshaven face framed by tangled elf locks of dark hair. He carries a tool bag over his shoulder. He clearly belongs to that class of people known as 'navvies', or to give them their correct title, navigators. His face marks him out as one of the much-despised nationality, the Irish. His thin body denotes that he hasn't eaten properly for a long time. It is probable he arrived in the city a few days ago, and has been working on one of the many demolition and reconstruction sites that have recently moved from the outskirts to the city centre.

Follow the young man's progress as he crosses the turbulent streets and enters a labyrinth of melancholy back alleys consisting of tumbling down properties wrapped in a mantle of soot. Here, the bricks are slimy and rough, the windows blind with dust, the doors cracked and rotten, the air faint, the light dim. The houses he passes have broken steps, and poles full of unsightly linen hang over the footways. Blinds, shutters, and curtains are all closed.

The young man pauses in front of a dismal grey door belonging to a cheap lodging-house that rents rooms to individuals on a daily or weekly basis. There is a sign in the window to that effect. He pushes the door open with the flat of his hand and steps through. The door closes behind him. A short while later he re-appears. The sign in the window said *No Irish*. He cannot read. The young man retraces his steps and begins to walk back the way he came, seeking somewhere to stay for the oncoming night. He walks and walks, passing parades of small shops, rows of brick terraces, wooden hoardings. Now the light is fading fast. He is beginning to feel unwell ~ maybe he caught something on the journey from Liverpool, maybe it's the lack of food, the digging, he does not know. He only knows that he cannot walk much further. He reaches a narrow, unlit alleyway, staggers along it, then slumps against a wall. High above his head, a lone bird is circling. He stares up at it, glassy-eyed. It will be the last thing on earth that he will see.

****

Monday morning, and the bells of the city are striking the half hour as Jack Cully, a senior detective in the Metropolitan Police, based at Scotland Yard, hurries along the street towards his place of work. He is accompanied by a young girl dressed in a smart navy pinafore and a white shirt and tie, a satchel bouncing on her back. The satchel contains her schoolbooks, three diligently completed pages of mathematical problems, an essay on the Romans, an apple and a packed lunch put up by her mother. Violet Cully is making the most of her scholarship to the prestigious

Westfield Girls' School: *'A College for the Education of Young Ladies'*, as its founder described it. She is enrolled in the preparatory class, one of the youngest pupils, but admitted on her entrance examination results and her confident interview with the formidable headmistress, Miss Dymphna Peak.

Every weekday, Violet sits at the front of the class, soaking up information like a sponge, frequently blindsiding her parents with facts she has absorbed during her lessons. Jack Cully is so proud of her achievements, though Emily sometimes worries that her clever daughter is in danger becoming, even at her tender age, a bit of a Bluestocking. She is trying hard to supplement Violet's head knowledge with some practical learning: sewing, cooking, ironing and how to turn sheets sides to middle.

Now the two reach 'farewell corner', the spot on their journey together where Violet goes one way to catch the omnibus that will take her to school, and Cully goes the opposite way to Scotland Yard. They go through the daily ritual ~ wishing each other a good day, warning each other to take care and stay out of trouble. Then Violet walks briskly off, chanting some rhyme about kings and queens, leaving Cully to wonder where the years have gone. It seems like only yesterday his daughter was a tiny child in smocked frocks, lifting her chubby arms to be picked up and set on his shoulders.

Shaking his head in bewilderment, Detective Inspector Cully continues on his journey. The change in his daughter is not the only thing to produce disconcerting thoughts. Since Detective Inspector Leo Stride, for so long the tetchy, idiosyncratic head of the Detective Division retired, change has been the order of the day. Stride, it is rumoured, is working on his memoirs and his garden. In his absence, his post has been filled temporarily by a succession of senior colleagues from various other divisions.

At last, and after some persuasion from his fellow officers, Inspector Lachlan Greig applied for and has just been appointed to the vacancy. A popular choice, Cully thinks, as he is much liked and respected by all who know and work with him. Cully shudders as he recalls the three months' tenure of Inspector James Frobisher, a caustic and unpleasant bully from an out-of- London police office, who nearly caused several good men to reconsider their position in the force. Chief Inspector Greig, as he is now, will have a steady hand on the tiller, and hopefully an aptitude for completing paperwork without throwing an inkpot at the opposite wall, a favourite reaction of his predecessor.

Cully himself had been approached at one time to see if he was interested in the promotion. But he is a street man. Always has been, always will be. He grew up on the streets, trained on the streets and the thought of being tied to a desk filling in endless forms for the Home Office and being berated by Whitehall mandarins fills him with horror. Elevation to detective inspector has afforded the family a little more money ~ much needed as Violet's demand for books grows weekly, but that is as far up the career ladder as Jack Cully intends to climb. He needs to be somewhere his feet can easily reach the cobbles.

Now, as he crosses Covent Garden piazza, Cully is unexpectedly hailed by the elderly coffee-stall holders whose morning task was to supply Detective Inspector Stride with a mug of dark treacly coffee. Even though Stride has not patronised their establishment for nearly a year, they still live in daily expectation of his reappearance. Cully sighs, as he steps towards them to remind them, once again, that their former regular customer has now retired and so won't be buying any more coffee from them.

"But we just seen him," the elderly man says, nodding enthusiastically in reply.

Cully frowns. "I think you must be mistaken," he responds.

"Din't we just see Mr Stride going into the p'lice house ten minutes back?" the man appeals to his wife, who wipes her hands on her grubby apron before agreeing. "I said to the wife: here he is again. I knew he couldn't keep away for long. Stands to reason. Busy man like Mr Stride."

Cully regards him dubiously. The couple have occupied the same pitch since time immemorial. He is not convinced they are still in possession of a complete set of mental faculties. "And he bought a cup of coffee from you, I suppose?" he says, a smile lurking at the corners of his mouth.

"Nah, we gave him a free one," the man says. "Least we could do after all this time. And we said we was glad to see him, and we hoped he was back for good. Place hasn't been the same without him."

Totally confused, Cully hurries towards Scotland Yard and pushes open the door. He greets the desk constable as he walks by, continues past Greig's office, then doubles back and enters. The room, which used to be a testament to his predecessor's 'file it on any available surface' strategy, is now alarmingly tidy. Whole areas of floor are visible. There is an absence of coffee mugs, the stains on the wall opposite the desk, marking where Stride hurled stuff when he felt particularly provoked by journalists, authority, or paperwork, have gone, and the plants on the windowsill are flourishing, even though the windows remain unwashed.

Chief Inspector Greig glances up from the report he is perusing.

"I don't suppose you've seen …?" Cully begins, frowning.

Greig grins. "He's down in the basement. I suspected he would be back before long. He said he was doing a bit of research for his memoirs. I told him it was fine as far as I was concerned. After all, it's not as if he is going to get involved with any investigations, is it?"

Cully nods. Actually, there is something almost comforting about the return of his old boss to the building. He remembers starting at Scotland Yard as a beat constable, working his way up to detective constable, detective sergeant and now detective inspector. Along the way, he could credit most of what he'd learned to Stride's advice and counsel. And a lot of what he'd chosen to ignore. He decides he will pay his former colleague a visit some time soon and see how he is getting on, as his own desk is remarkably empty at the moment.

****

Meanwhile, Felix Lawrence, recently arrived back in England, and appointed a general surgeon at the London Hospital, is engaged in a tricky dissection process when the bell rings. He looks up from his plate, where he is removing the fat from a slice of bacon with a serrated knife. It is too early for any private patients to be calling. And he is pretty sure he isn't expecting any other callers. He waits for his man to answer, his knife poised above the plate, ears straining to hear the conversation taking place on the other side of the door.

As he waits, Lawrence thinks back to his previous employment. He recalls the porter pushing his trunk up the gangplank and installing him in the first-class cabin. Fresh from medical school, and eager not to settle down quite yet, he had obtained the post of ship's doctor on the Oxus, bound for the Far East.

His quarters then were more luxurious than his bachelor rooms now, he reflects ruefully. He wore a white uniform with five gold stripes that marked him out as the doctor. He took orders only from the captain, at whose table he dined. He was treated with the utmost respect by crew and passengers alike. And he was not expected to be at the beck and call of everyone. But the ill-health of his mother has recalled him back to England. Sadly. Lawrence likes adventure, combined with luxury and high living. He does not intend to stay in London for long. Once she has departed this mortal coil, he will depart this gloomy city and the cold inhospitable country for somewhere more exotic.

A few moments later, the servant knocks and enters. Following him is an imposing elderly man with grey hair, a gold-topped walking stick and a worried expression. At the sight of him, Lawrence rises to his feet instantly, his breakfast forgotten. "Sir Charles? What brings you here at this time of the morning? Not bad news, I hope?"

Sir Charles Trelawny, renowned senior surgeon, and Board Member at the London Hospital, passes the brim of his well-brushed silk top hat between his trembling fingers. Looks at the mantelpiece. Clears his throat. "I need you to accompany me to the hospital, Felix. At once, if you can. There is something that … well … I won't prejudge your opinion. Suffice to say, you are recently returned from the Far East, and so might be able to shed some light on it. My carriage is waiting at the door."

Now thoroughly alarmed, Felix Lawrence abandons his meal and his truculence, orders the servant to fetch his coat, hat, and gloves, and accompanies his companion out into the street, where a shiny burgundy brougham attends. The two men climb into the carriage, and are driven swiftly away, arriving a short while later at Whitechapel Road. The carriage stops outside the rear entrance to the hospital, where they alight. Trelawny beckons his companion to follow him, placing a finger to his lips to indicate that they must remain silent.

Mystified, but his curiosity growing by the second, Felix Lawrence passes through the back entrance to the hospital, where deliveries are received, and the detritus removed. He steps over a pile of laundry sacks and round some brass cylinders with rubber pipes extruding from their tops.

His companion takes a key from the pocket of his frock coat and unlocks a door. He beckons Lawrence to follow. They enter a small dimly-lit room, the walls whitewashed. It is windowless and the air smells of damp and disuse. At the centre is a steel table, on top of which lies something wrapped in a white cloth. From where he is standing, Lawrence sees dark blood stains dotting the covering.

"The man you are about to view was found in the rear alley in the early hours of the morning. A porter discovered him. He was dead, but his condition ~ which I am about to display to you, has caused such alarm that it was decided to move him directly to an isolated room where he couldn't come into contact with anybody else." Trelawny approaches the table and carefully, at arms' length and using his walking stick, twitches back the white covering.

Lawrence looks down, feeling the room swim around him. For a second, he has the sensation of falling. The corpse's face is grey-white, and the tips of the fingers are black ~ unmistakeable signs of necrotization. More alarming still are the black swellings on his neck. The signs are unmistakeable.

For a long, long moment, the two men stand side by side, staring at the monstrous spectacle in front of them. Neither speaks. It is as if death has announced itself by silencing their tongues. The silence travels back and forth between them. Eventually Lawrence speaks: "I have seen this on my travels," he says, "China was just recovering from such an outbreak that had killed millions when I left. Poor soul. It is a vile disease, and a dreadful way to die, for there is no known cure." He steps back, staring at Trelawny in fear. "And it is contagious. Every person who came into contact with this man must be traced. They will need to go into isolation at once."

A meaningful look passes between them.

"Have you notified the authorities?" Lawrence asks.

Trelawney bites his lower lip. "You are right. Yes, of course you are right. We should do that. Fortunately, I used to know one of the officers in the Detective Division based at Scotland Yard. I shall write to him at once seeking the best way forward," he shudders. "I never thought to see an example of this once again in London. Certainly not in my lifetime. It is as if some evil ghost from the past has risen up out of the grave."

"And while we await his response?" Lawrence inquires. "We should dispose of the body as quickly as we can, surely?"

Trelawney pulls a face. "We should indeed. Though we will have to show the officials the corpse. Briefly. I suggest that we keep this room locked in the meantime. Nobody should go in; it is too much of a risk. I will arrange with the porters for a guard upon the door." He turns worried eyes upon his companion. "You do not remember the cholera outbreak ~ you would have been a mere boy, but I recall it vividly. We had to take on extra staff to cope with demand. Every bed, every ward was full, and we were stretched to the utmost. If this should get out, Felix, to the newspapers for instance, think of the reputation of the hospital! The Grocers' Company wing is due to be completed in the next few years. How will we manage if they withdraw funding?"

"Then we must do all in our power to ensure that it does not," Felix Lawrence says calmly, taking the older man's arm and leading him away. "And we must also hope that this is an isolated incident. The consequences are just too horrific to contemplate."

****

Ex-Detective Inspector Leo Stride stands in the centre of the dimly lit basement, surveying the wooden shelves of box files and tin trunks that hold the reports and tangible evidence of past investigations. He has a notebook, a pencil, and an expression of deep content on his face. The past months have been a bit of an endurance. Finally acceding to his wife's constant requests that he should retire and spend more time at home, it has been a tad galling to discover, once he had quit, that she actually preferred him elsewhere.

Since leaving Scotland Yard, Stride has painted the scullery and the kitchen, and laid new linoleum in the hallway. That seems to be the extent of his usefulness. Mrs Stride, unbeknown to him, always entertains various groups of church and charity ladies on a regular basis in the afternoons, an activity that required him, as a mere male, to vacate the matrimonial home. Then there were her morning calls to the butcher, baker, and candlestick maker, all of which she preferred to perform solo. If he was lucky, he managed to snatch some brief quality time during supper, but as it usually consisted of a list of activities that required his attention or his absence, it hardly counted.

Now, as he breathes in the rarified dust-laden air of the basement, Stride sighs happily. This is his world. This is where he belongs, surrounded by the written evidence of hundreds of crimes and misdemeanours. His eye runs down the meticulously labelled files: The Vestry Poisoning, The Four Cherry Stones, The Yellow Parasol Murders, The Romanian Countess ~ a shudder goes down his spine as he reads that one. Stride still remembers the case vividly: the image of the Countess' body impaled upon the iron railings outside her house still occasionally returns to haunt his dreams. He lifts a couple of box files down and takes them to the table. Then he gets out the notebook and pencil, and prepares to re-enter the murky gaslit purlieus of his former life.

Time passes. As soon as his pocket watch signals midday, Stride puts down his pencil, closes up his notebook and leaves Scotland Yard. He makes his way to a certain dark, low-ceilinged hostelry off Fleet Street, known colloquially as Sally's Chop House after the eponymous owner. It was where, in his days of legitimate employment, he liked to dine. He greets the waitering staff, then weaves between the tables until he reaches the back booth where he always used to sit; fortuitously it is empty, though crumbs and spilt ale on the wooden table bear evidence of previous occupants.

Stride sits down, and as if he has been awaiting his reappearance, Sally materialises from the background, wearing his food-stained apron and a cautious expression.

"Why, it's Mr Stride, well I never! Here you are again. Wot a surprise. I fort you'd retired from the policing business some time back," he says, trying to imbue the greeting with as much enthusiasm as he can fake.

The relationship between Stride, detective and customer, and Sally, chop-house owner, and ex-criminal, has always been a complex affair, although Stride has never managed to pick up on the subtle nuances of it. As far as Sally is concerned, this particular customer always pays the bill, which he never queries, and doesn't attempt to leave with cutlery in his pocket, but he still gives off an aura of policeman, which other customers find off-putting. After all, you don't want to be eating your midday meal with the remembrances of crimes committed hovering in the air around you.

"I'm just doing a bit of research, Sally," Stride tells him cheerfully. "Investigating my investigations, as it were. I'm writing my memoirs for publication, you see. I call it *'The Life and Legacy of a London Detective'* ~ just a temporary title so far, you understand. Always good to revisit the past, don't you think?"

Sally's past consists of various journeys through the prison system, beginning at age 10, punctuated by numerous failed enterprises involving the illegally obtained goods of others, and sporadic acts of extreme violence in the boxing ring. He has absolutely no intention of revisiting it. Ever. However, assuming a tenuously interested expression, he nods, because the customer has to be accommodated, and the sooner Stride gets his food, the sooner he will have eaten it and left.

"Your usual, is it then, Mr Stride?"

Stride considers the question. "Ah, well. Perhaps, as this is somewhat of an occasion, I might push the boat out a bit, Sally. I will have a plate of your finest chops, in gravy. And a baked potato to accompany them. And a glass of beer."

"Right you are, Mr Stride, just as you wish; fetching it now," Sally says, hurrying off to organise the meal. It is exactly what Stride has always ordered, but as revisiting the past is not something he cares to do, he isn't going to enlighten him.

Stride tucks into his food with gusto, his mind spinning as he mulls over all the case reports he has read through earlier. He is just scraping his plate and contemplating the work that lies ahead of him, when he hears his name being called and looking up, he sees a familiar figure making his way towards him.

****

While Stride is enjoying his celebratory luncheon, a letter is brought in to the front desk of Scotland Yard. It is addressed to Detective Inspector L. Stride, Detective Division and marked 'Urgent. Reply needed at once.' The bearer of the missive, a stout man who wears a uniform indicating that he is one of the ancillary staff at the London Hospital, deposits the letter and leans on the desk, breathing loudly.

"Urgent, they said," he puffs, indicating the superscript. "Gotta be read as soon as. Messenger to wait, they said."

The desk constable takes the letter, reads the addressee, and hands it over to a passing officer. "Take this to Mr Greig. He'll know what to do," he says.

The officer conveys the communication to Lachlan Greig's office and places it on his desk. Then he stands back awaiting further orders. Greig turns the letter over a couple of times, frowns, then checks the time. He rises. "Thank you, officer. You can leave this with me. I think I know where to find Mr Stride."

Greig dons his hat and walks the short distance to the Chop House where, as he suspected, Stride is just finishing his meal. He greets him, slides into the opposite seat, and places the letter on the table. "This came for you while you were out," he says. "I presume the writer does not know you have now retired."

Stride wipes his knife on his plate and uses it to slit open the envelope. He takes out a carefully folded sheet of good quality writing paper and reads. As he does so, the frown lines between his brows deepen. Greig sits in silence, waiting for him to finish. Eventually, Stride looks up. He pushes the letter across the table. "You'd better read this," he says. "It sounds serious."

Greig scans the letter, then gets to his feet. "I shall take a cab to the hospital and see what's afoot," he says.

"I'll accompany you then, if I may," Stride says, eagerly gathering his things together.

There is a pause.

"Really? I don't see …"

"The letter was addressed to me," Stride observes.

Biting back a response, Greig indicates that in that case, they should leave at once. Stride throws some coins onto the table and together the two go in search of a cab, leaving Sally to pocket the money and heave a sigh of relief. One detective is bad enough. Two of the blighters is pushing it.

A short ride through the midday traffic, and the cab drops Stride and Greig outside the London Hospital. They mount the steps and enter the atrium, where various medical students are milling around, discussing important issues like the best place to dine and the price and location of the cheapest beer. Greig goes up to the desk, and requests to see Sir Charles Trelawney. The hospital official regards him suspiciously.

"And what would this be about, may I inquire? Sir Charles is a very h'important man in these parts."

Greig produces Stride's letter. "I think you will find he has time to see us. Now, please convey the information that we are here, at once."

The porter glances at the piece of paper, then hurries off, returning a short while later in the company of Sir Charles Trelawney and a much younger man. There is a moment's awkward pause while the senior surgeon fails to recognise Stride (it has been several years since they last met). Eventually, contact is made, the companion is introduced as Felix Lawrence, a junior colleague, and, at his indication, the two men follow them into the back recesses of the hospital, down a flight of stone steps, and along a badly lit corridor until they halt in front of a door. The senior surgeon has remained silent throughout the journey. Now he turns to face them.

"Gentlemen," he says, "you are about to witness a sight that I never thought to see in my lifetime. In seeking your advice as to the best course to pursue, I must also demand that you do not breathe a word of it to anybody outside this hospital. In particular, nobody from any of the newspapers must find out. I cannot overemphasize this enough."

Sir Charles takes a key from his waistcoat pocket and unlocks the door. "I advise you both not to enter fully into this room," he says. "We have diagnosed what has befallen the individual. Your presence is requested in your official capacity as officers of the crown, to alert you to our discovery and also to seek some advice as to how we should progress."

He opens the door. The sickly-sweet smell of decaying flesh, mixed with something chemical leaches out. Stride peers over his colleague's shoulder at the body on the hospital gurney, then takes out his handkerchief and buries his nose into it. The sight and smell are worse than anything he encountered in his career, and his entanglements with Robertson, the dour, sarcastic police surgeon. He turns away. The surgeon closes the door and re-locks it.

"We are keeping people well away from this area, for obvious reasons," he says, quietly. He takes them to the end of the corridor and opens a low door leading to a short alleyway. At the end of the alleyway, carriages and people pass by.

"This is where the body was discovered last night," Felix Laurence says. "I have made inquiries of the night porter, but he does not recall anyone ringing the bell. The man was found outside the door at the change of staff. He has been handled with extreme care by a few trustworthy medical people, well protected. Obviously, there cannot be an autopsy, given the nature of the disease. My question is: can we, the hospital authorities, now dispose of the body, as quickly as possible, having reported it to you?"

Greig walks a few paces along the alleyway, deep in contemplation. "You have no idea who the man was?" he says, walking back.

Trelawny shakes his head. "We think from his clothes and general bodily appearance he was a manual labourer. Possibly Irish. He certainly wasn't well fed. We found no money and no personal objects, other than some tools of his trade."

Greig gets out his notebook and begins writing. "On the one hand, we must make every attempt to trace the man's immediate family. On the other hand, if we go public with the revelation that he has died of this disease, we will have the whole of London scared out of its wits," he says thoughtfully. "We will have to be extremely circumspect. I suggest an innocuous 'Missing Persons' advertisement might be in order, and we will alert our police offices accordingly. Let us see if anybody recognises a description of him and can tell us where he might have laboured.

"I think you should also inform your colleagues at other London hospitals and private clinics ~ they need to be on the lookout for anybody presenting with similar symptoms, although let us fervently hope nobody does." He closes his notebook. "I won't authorise a coroner's inquest for obvious reasons, but I invite you to send me a medical report, which I will forward to the coroner's office and to the Home Office."

Sir Charles indicates his agreement. "Thank you. We will accede to your request. But may I express my opinion again: God forbid that the news of this gets out."

"Indeed so," Greig's expression is solemn. "And let us also hope that this poor unfortunate is the only victim."

Meanwhile, back in the foyer of the hospital, the porter has returned to his official duties, which now involve clearing the atrium of noisy students. But while he bustles around doing crowd dispersal, his mind is elsewhere. The top hospital medic. sent an urgent letter to Scotland Yard. Two detectives appeared as a result. Something serious must be going on. And if he suspects something serious is going on, how is he going to find out exactly how serious it is, and having found out, what is he going to do with the information?

****

Fast forward a couple of hours. At her consulting rooms in 122A Baker Street, Miss Lucy Landseer, London's finest (and only) female private investigator is about to 'put up the shutters for the day', as she likes to think of it. She has been engaged upon her current case since early morning: an investigation into a suspected adultery, involving hours of patient surveillance outside one of London's smarter blocks of flats. It has, however, finally yielded the desired result, and she has just written to her female client to inform her of the findings.

She is packing away her notebook, not expecting any new business to arrive, so the unexpected step on the stair, and the tentative knock at her door comes as somewhat of a surprise. Lucy sets down her satchel and goes to open the door, revealing a veiled woman standing on the landing. She makes a quick assessment of her visitor's well-cut dress, silk mantle and bonnet, and places her into the class known as well-bred gentlewoman. The woman takes a small gold-rimmed pasteboard calling card from her reticule and hands it to Lucy.

"I am not accustomed to visiting private detectives," she says, "especially at this hour of the day, but the situation in which I find myself demands that I take unusual steps to rectify. I have made inquiries, and your name has been suggested as one who is both discreet and efficient."

Lucy bows her head. "I hope I am. Please come in, Miss Broxton. If you would like to take a seat, just there, I am at your disposal. Everything you tell me goes no further than these four walls." Lucy unpacks her notebook and pencil, then settles herself on the other side of the desk. And waits.

The visitor raises her veil. She is in middle age, her grey-streaked hair pulled back from a broad forehead. No beauty, she is stout of figure, and has strongly marked, swarthy features: thick eyebrows, a square jaw, a mouth set and determined. Not the sort of person to tolerate fools gladly, Lucy thinks. Miss Broxton carefully removes her gloves, one finger at a time, straightens them, and lays them on her lap. She looks up.

"Before I embark upon the reason for my visit, I feel I must explain to you that I come from a good, very respectable county family. We can trace our ancestors back to the Normans. Our family seat is in Suffolk. Over the centuries, there have been Broxtons in the Judiciary and in the City. One of our number is currently a member of the House of Lords."

"I understand," Lucy says.

"However, my particular branch of the family tree is a cadet branch. And we have, how can I put it, grown, and developed in an unusual manner. I see you do not follow me, Miss Landseer. Let me clarify. Whereas it is customary for the oldest son in a family to inherit, in our case, due to a legal anomaly, all the wealth, property and land devolves upon a member of the female line. My mother bequeathed the family wealth to my sister, who, although younger, was the more likely to marry and produce a female heir in her turn. By rights, she should hand it down to her daughter." The visitor pauses, looking over Lucy's shoulder at the portrait of the forbidding matron that hangs behind her desk, but who is not a family member, having been purchased in a little art shop opposite the British Museum.

"Ah. I see. Do I gather that there is no daughter to inherit?" Lucy asks.

The visitor shoots her a sharp glance from under the forbidding eyebrows. "Oh, there is indeed a female child," she says. "Or at least, as far as we know, there *was* one." She pauses. "I am told that discretion is your watchword, Miss Landseer. The story I am about to relate requires the utmost discretion upon your part. Can I be assured of that?"

Lucy nods. "Indeed, you can, Miss Broxton. Pray proceed with your story. I will make notes if you do not mind. They will help me to remember the important details."

"Then I shall commence. Know that my sister and I had the best of upbringings: we had tutors, ponies; we had dancing lessons, etiquette lessons; we had loving parents whose only desire was to ensure we were brought up as young gentlewomen. Our destiny was to marry well. But by the age of sixteen, it was already apparent that I, at least, did not possess the necessary attributes to attract a suitor ~ oh, you may spare me the look of sympathy, Miss Landseer. To me it was a great relief. The company of vapid young men bored me rigid. The setting forth of my charms, like some huckster, with the sole intent of hooking a husband reminded me of the efforts of a fisherman who places a worm on the end of a line to entice some hapless fish. And I had no intention of being that worm. To my parents' consternation, I decided to apply to a college with the intention of studying for a teaching qualification. Yes, I became what society scornfully calls a 'Bluestocking'. But now, should my circumstances alter, I have the ability to obtain paid employment, so will never be reliant upon any man for my daily bread.

"Meanwhile my younger sister Margaret was growing into a veritable beauty. By fifteen, she was already known as the 'Belle of the County'. To my parents' delight, she 'came out' to a successful Season. The mantelpiece of the rented London house was full of invitation cards to balls, evening parties and picnics. She was the toast of the town. Young men of good breeding and class flocked to the door. My parents hoped she would be engaged by Christmas. They returned home full of plans and hopes.

"Alas, it rapidly became apparent that something was wrong. As the days went by, Margaret became more and more withdrawn. Finally, she took to her room. And that was where she remained, refusing to come down for meals, requesting that her food was sent up on trays. This went on for some time. My parents wrote desperate letters to me ~ I was away from the family house, teaching at a girls' school. However, when term finished, I returned home. I went straight up to my sister's room, and without knocking, I entered. Margaret was standing by the window, wearing a loose gown. It was immediately obvious to me why she had kept herself secluded and private and what was wrong with her. My poor sister, Miss Landseer, was expecting a child."

The visitor drops her gaze to her lap. Silence fills the room. Lucy's pen pauses. She makes a conscious effort to keep her expression neutral. Miss Broxton lifts her head and stares straight at her, as if assessing her reaction to the shocking revelation. Then, satisfied by the lack of any judgement visible in Lucy's eyes, she continues.

"My sister threw herself at my feet and burst into tears. I sat her on the bed, put my arms around her, and let her cry upon my breast as she told me the sorry tale. A young marquis, flattery and billet-doux, carriage-rides, kisses and promises, I need not go into details. Enough to say that having had his way with her, he hurriedly left London for the continent and has never been heard of again. 'Now I am ruined, dear sister. I cannot disgrace my family,' my poor sister sobbed. 'I have decided to make my way to London and throw myself into the river Thames'. This was her desperate plan. Of course, I could not allow it. I told her I would think of a better way, and after cogitating all night, I decided the best thing would be to take her to London with me. We'd rent a small room in some back street, and when the birth happened, the child could be placed in an institution for such infants. How we persuaded my parents of this course of action is not part of my story. Suffice to say they furnished us with sufficient funds to provide us with board and lodgings in Camden Town. I returned to work. My sister kept herself secluded. And in time, a baby was born. It was a girl.

"A few days after its birth, I set out alone to dispose of the infant. It was a spring evening; the moon was full, and the sky covered with light clouds. The baby was well wrapped up in a shawl, so as not to arouse suspicion. To the curious passer-by, it looked as if I was carrying a small bundle of washing. I was myself heavily veiled. I walked to the nearest cab stand and asked the cabman to take me to an Asylum for Female Orphans. I had made a prior survey of local orphanages and institutions for the care of foundlings of both sexes, and had chosen this particular one for the child, should it be female, as it took in infant girls whose mothers were unable to care for them, but who belonged to a respectable social class.

"My sister had placed a jewelled locket in the shawl wrapped around the baby. I left the child upon the step of the chosen institution and made my way back to our lodgings on foot. And so, the child passed out of our hands, never to be heard of again."

The client pauses. Lucy nods in what she hopes is a 'continue, I am listening' way. Miss Broxton adjusts her gloves. Then resumes her narrative.

"Well, the years went by, but if we hoped my sister might return to her former self, it was not to be. A deep melancholy settled upon her, driving all idea of marriage and her own family out of the picture. My parents consulted every medical expert they could find: all said the same thing ~ give her time, she will recover. But she showed no sign of any recovery. Her bright looks faded. And of course, no young men were interested in courting a semi-invalid.

"And now, with the lack of a female heir, we are faced with the prospect of losing our family home and our entire inheritance as well. So, we have decided upon a course of action. It is also precipitated by a letter from the lawyer acting for Mr Jasper Broxton, our cousin, reminding us of his claim upon our inheritance. He is a bully, and we feel powerless to defend ourselves. My sister's health is always delicate; the doctors have now said there is nothing more they can do for her. Obviously, I have no offspring to inherit. So, you see, we wish you, Miss Landseer, to find the girl for us, and as quickly as it is possible."

After her client has left, Lucy Landseer makes her way back to the house she rents with her Cambridge professor. In her satchel is a banker's draft on Miss Broxton's city bank. Plus her address and that of the female orphanage. Lucy is walking home, as she finds it a good way of ordering her thoughts. She is frowning as she walks. She did not take to the woman. There was something cold about her. Something lacking. She remembers a similar investigation she had taken on some time ago: a father, desperate to track down his son and daughter after quitting the country to make a life for them in America.

Her mind throws up an image of his face, the suffering in his eyes. It was clear that the man loved his children and would do anything to be reunited. Yes ~ that was what was itching at her brain: the word love. To Miss Broxton, it seemed that the babe was initially an inconvenience, to be disposed of. Now, the child was a commodity to be acquired.

Lucy pulls a wry mouth. She had done her very best to help her former client, but in the end, she had to concede defeat. It had hurt. It still did whenever her thoughts strayed to the case. She decides that, for his sake, she will set aside her own feelings, put her shoulder to the wheel and redeem herself. Besides, she reminds herself, as she reaches her own front door and pulls the key from her coat pocket, she is not paid to like her clients, only to help them to a successful resolution of their difficulties.

****

Later that evening. A small backstreet hostelry called the Master's Arms, but better known to its regulars as 'Jake's' after the landlord, who used to be a pugilist in his youth and still could throw unruly customers out into the fetid alleyway at the back of the pub with one hand tied behind his back (allegedly). It is the type of public house that smells of unwashed humanity, stale cabbage, spilt beer and drains; the sort of place that, if it ever acquired an entry in *Bradshaw's Illustrated Handbook to London and its Environs (1870 ed.)*, would probably get the comment: 'Best avoided'.

Tonight however, two men have chosen to patronise its dimly-lit public bar. They sit in a dark corner ~ although most of this particular public house consists of dark corners. On the table before them, two pint pots. One of the men is the hospital porter we encountered earlier, now no longer in his brown overalls. His companion wears a loud check overcoat with a greasy velvet collar, a canary-yellow scarf, and a cloth cap. His smile reminds one of a crocodile lurking in the shallows, awaiting the approach of an unwary swimmer.

"Right then, squire," he says, whipping out a notebook and pencil from some inner pocket,

"Watchoo got for me tonight? Unexpected dead body brought in by mysterious individuals?"

The porter glances furtively all around, a gesture that always encourages everyone within earshot to lower their voices, assume a nonchalant expression, and lean in attentively.

"It's like this, Mr Dandy sir," he says, "I was in the atrium, performing my reg'lar duties like I always do, when two detectives from Scotland Yard approached ..."

"Describe them," interrupts the chief reporter on *The Inquirer*, his gaze narrowing.

"One was a tall man, clean shaven, reddish hair ..."

"Greig," the reporter murmurs. "I know him. Go on ..."

"The other man was much older. Bit shabby looking. Walrus moustache, grey hair."

The reporter utters an exclamation. "Stride! I never! I thought the bugger had retired. It must be something pretty serious if they've had to call him in. Now that's worth a pint in itself. Go on ..."

"Well," the porter says, a smug expression on his face because he senses he has imparted something important, although he hasn't a clue what it is, "the two Scotland Yarders went straight to the back of the 'orspital, where the mortuary is located. They went wiv Sir Charles, who is the top surgeon. They went to the mortuary, like I said, but ..." he leans forward, "they didn't come back."

Dandy frowns. "You mean they are still down there?"

"Nah, nah. I means that once they'd seen it, they left by the rear entrance. So whatever it was, they didn't want to be seen leaving the 'orspital. Anyway, later, when it was quiet like, I took a trip down there to see if I could work out what was going on."

Dandy fixes his eyes on his companion's face. "And what did you discover?"

"Well, there was a constable at the end of the corridor, what I hadn't seen arrive, and I was told I couldn't go no further. In all the years wot I've worked at that 'orspital, I ain't never seen the like of that. The p'liceman was there all afternoon, and only left just afore I came off my shift. And when I took a stroll down the corridor, the small mortuary door was locked."

"I see," Dandy nods, though at the moment, it is about as clear as Thames mud to him. "And what do YOU think is going on?"

The porter takes a long pull at his pint, wipes his mouth on the back of his jacket sleeve. "I reckon there's some skulduggery afoot. Why was them detectives sent for? Why did they leave by the back way? And why was there p'lice outside one of the mortuary rooms for the rest of the day? And then there wasn't. What was in that room that nobody wanted anybody else to know about, eh?"

What indeed, thinks Richard Dandy, chief reporter on *The Inquirer* ~ the paper that speaks for the Man in the Street, as it styles itself. But he knows that what he has been told is only the first link in the tale. The hospital porter is useful, but only in a limited way. Nevertheless, he has supplied Dandy with some interesting details and preliminary information. Which he can now go on to explore. He tosses back the last of his pint and rises to his feet. Touching his cap to the porter, he crosses the bar floor and goes out into the night. Tomorrow, Fleet Street's finest will start pulling a few threads to see what unravels.

****

Regent's Park was once part of the transformation of London into a city that would, its architects believed, stir the pride, and present to the world the taste and humanity, as well as the wealth and power of the British nation. Regent's Park, its noble terraces springing up as if by magic around the park itself with its 543 acres, was meant to represent *'a union of architectural beauty on a scale of greater magnificence than can be found in any other place'* (Quarterly Journal, 1827).

Dirty alleys, dingy courts and squalid dens of misery and crime were torn down, to be replaced by stately streets, elegant mansions and sweeping terraces, their pillared and white stuccoed frontages purportedly the abode of the aristocracy. Alas, by the time of this narrative, the bright white paintwork has faded, the statuary is dilapidated, plaster is peeling off the walls and social decay is everywhere.

The same decay outwith its walls is echoed within, and no more so than the mid-terrace property rented by Jasper Broxton, his wife Avice, son Shedleigh and daughter Johanna. Jasper Broxton, of Broxton Business Investment & Financial Services, likes to describe himself as a financial entrepreneur and investment expert, which translates as someone who persuades gullible people to give him sums of money upon the premise of making more sums of money in the future. Some of which might trickle down to them.

Currently, this *modus operandi* is sputtering, as the investments are not yielding the profit he has anticipated, plus the business isn't attracting enough new clients to use their money to reimburse earlier ones, which is how Broxton likes to operate. Retrenchments have had to be made domestically. A couple of servants have been 'let go'. A new dress for his wife has been cancelled. Thus, the family gathered round the breakfast table on this fine morning, are in a gloomy mood. This has just been made worse by a letter from Shedleigh's headmaster, reminding Mr Broxton that the termly fees for his board and education are late. Angrily, he holds up a piece of toast.

"Faugh! Why is Cook unable to make toast without burning it?" he snarls.

Avice Broxton narrows her pale eyes and bites her lower lip. She is still smarting over the cancellation of her summer dress. Resentment seeps from her like some sullen and ominous perfume. "Perhaps if we paid her a decent wage, she might produce better food?" she suggests acidly.

Broxton ignores this. He attacks the dry burnt offering with his knife, smearing it viciously in butter. Meanwhile thirteen-year-old Johanna Broxton bends over her plate, shovelling in bacon, watery eggs, and flabby bread as fast as she can. She is a big fleshy girl, with the same dark brows and sallow complexion as her aunt. Her school uniform strains at the seams, and her dark hair, which is put into curling rags every night, hangs limply down either side of her face. Every morning, she piles ruthlessly into the breakfast menu on offer, stuffing as much as she can down her before she has to leave for school. There is never enough to eat, as her parents are so stingy. Keeping up appearances requires cutting back on things like food.

"Johanna ~ you are gobbling again!" her mother says sternly. "You won't attract a husband with table manners like that!"

Johanna mutters something unrepeatable.

"You may leave the table," her mother says, ignoring it. "The carriage will be waiting. Have a good day at school. Study hard. You are lucky your father is paying for you to have an education. I did not have an education when I was growing up. And may I take the opportunity to say we were not overly-impressed with your last term's report. Both your father and I hope you will improve. Shedleigh is now third in his class, and he has been picked for the rugby team."

Seething with resentment, Johanna Broxton slouches out of the breakfast room. In the hallway, she grabs her coat, book bag and school hat. Without a word of thanks to the parlour maid, she bundles through the opened front door and gets into the carriage, which bears the family coat of arms on the door. Or rather, what Jasper Broxton imagines the family coat of arms might look like if it actually existed. The carriage is one of the few things he has chosen not to dispense with. Appearance is all-important in the world of high (or dodgy) finance.

After wending its way through the busy morning traffic, the carriage eventually arrives at the entrance of her girls' school, where Johanna is decanted unceremoniously onto the pavement. She approaches the ornate iron gates. A couple of younger pupils are standing outside, comparing homework. She recognises them as scholarship pupils, (her cash-conscious parents put her in for a scholarship; she didn't get it. Another source of grievance).

"Get out of my way, you stupid charity brats," she hisses, barging straight through, her elbows knocking their books out of their hands.

Johanna Broxton mounts the steps leading into the building. Meanwhile, Violet Cully and her friend May Higgins pick up their books from the pavement, dust them off and eye her departing figure thoughtfully.

"My father says you have to stand up to bullies," Violet remarks.

"She's bigger than us though," May observes gloomily. "A lot bigger."

"All the more reason. And she might be bigger and older, but we are much cleverer, aren't we? Come on, we mustn't be late for assembly."

Violet Cully links her arm through her friend's arm and together, the two enter the hallowed portals and make their way to the Assembly Hall, a room so completely panelled in dark wood it is like sitting in a cigar box. As her face endures the bible reading, and singing the school song (twelve verses in Latin celebrating the advantages of female education, and composed when the lady founders were sharing a cottage in the Lake District), Violet's busy brain is working on a variety of scenarios in which she and May defeat their enemy and are declared heroines by their classmates.

Meanwhile Johanna Broxton, sitting four rows behind them, is planning how to persuade various younger students to part with any sweets or cakes in their possession, without leaving bruisage for which she might be held accountable, while at the same time mentally rehearsing her excuses for not completing her various homework assignments.

****

A plan, or something similar, is also being hatched by Johanna's mother, Avice Broxton. As soon as her husband and daughter have left for their various destinations, she gets up from the breakfast table, indicating to the maid that she is free to clear it. Her first port of call is the study. Her husband keeps it locked, but she has had the key copied.

Seating herself behind his desk, she starts to go through his personal correspondence, always taking care to keep it in exactly the same order as she found it. She learns that Shedleigh's headmaster will send the boy home unless the fees are paid forthwith. She also learns that various people, a few of them former friends, are threatening to contact the police over the refusal of her husband's company (Broxton Business Investment & Financial Services) to return their money. And there is a pawn ticket for some of the family silver. She hasn't seen that before.

After carefully replacing everything on the desk and locking the study door once more, Avice goes upstairs to her dressing room to make preparations. As she sits at her dressing table, brushing and arranging her thin fair hair (the lady's maid was the first to be let go), she runs through a mental inventory of the Broxton land and properties ~ all currently in the possession of her husband's sickly cousin. There is Broxton Hall (eight bedrooms, conservatory, gravel driveway, carriage house, paddock, forty acres of garden with ornamental pond, orangery, and orchard), currently let. There is Broxton Hall Farm, currently let. Broxton Woods ~ common land, for now. Plus, of course, the rental income from the Broxton Arms, and various village shops and cottages.

It all amounts to school fees paid, dresses made, staff rehired, new furnishings and a life of unlimited luxury for the foreseeable future. The only thing standing in her way is that sickly young woman. Angrily, she thrusts a couple of combs into her hair. Last night, she had the dream again, the one where she is standing behind Margaret Broxton who is herself standing on the edge of a cliff. She reaches out her hand, and in a moment, Margaret is gone. She makes no sound. Avice closes her eyes. I am a good person. I love my family, she repeats.

Some time later, after visiting the kitchen and telling the cook to make last night's joint into rissoles, Avice leaves the house. She walks down Regent's Street, her head held high, her step determined. Her face is set in a grim expression. At the end of the street, she catches an omnibus, which drops her at the corner of the road where Margaret Broxton and her ugly older sister reside. Avice walks a few yards, then slides into a doorway opposite. Why does she choose to live here? she wonders. Given all the money the sisters have at their disposal, they could easily rent a property in one of the fashionable areas. And they don't even keep a carriage.

She stares at the house. The blinds are drawn down. A spatter of rain falls from the sooty sky. Avice pulls her shawl and her resentment closer to her. She sends black darts of hatred towards the first-floor window behind whose shuttered glass she imagines the invalid Margaret Broxton (whom she has never met), wearing a silk peignoir, sitting in her white four poster bed, her skin tallow-coloured, her arms and wrists like sticks, dining on fine viands. Meanwhile, her family has nothing. (Not quite true, but when you are turning a sense of grievance into a full-time career, facts are always the first casualties.)

The rain continues to fall. The blinds remain down. Nobody leaves the house. Nobody arrives at the house. Avice goes on watching. She will remain in position until the church bells chime midday. Then she will depart. In the afternoon, she has to sit on a church committee for the Salvation and Ultimate Betterment of Destitute and Despondent Female Vagrants. Because in her social position, it is expected of her. Now, she waits and watches, seething internally. As the clock strikes the hour of departure, and she steps out of the doorway into the rain, she wonders bitterly how soon it will be before she joins the desperate female vagrants too.

****

Meanwhile, Chief Inspector Lachlan Greig, newly appointed head of the Detective Division of Scotland Yard, is staring down at the slew of morning papers that have been placed on his desk. His eye has been irresistibly drawn to the front-page banner headline in *The Inquirer*:

DEADLY DISEASE DETECTED IN DEAD MAN!
Hospital Experts Baffled! Is London In The Grip Of A Fatal Outbreak?

There follows, under the familiar by-line of R. Dandy (Chief Reporter) several paragraphs of stunningly hyperbolic and lurid prose that border not only upon the completely inaccurate but steps boldly into the practically libellous. Greig feels his heart sink. How on earth had Dandy Dick got hold of the story? From whom? Greig reaches for his notepad and begins to draft an angry letter to the editor. This reckless mendacity cannot be allowed to spread further. It could start the mass panic that the surgeons at the London Hospital were worried about.

As he reaches the end of his missive, the door to his office opens and Stride enters. "Ah, I see you have read it," he says, indicating the newspaper. "The imagination of our penny-a-liner hacks never ceases to amaze."

Greig nods, grim-faced. He has been particularly stung by Dandy Dick's suggestion that he, the head of the Detective Division, was so baffled by the deadly disease about to ravish the city, that he's had to call in his predecessor to help.

"It must be somebody who works in the hospital," Stride says, nodding sagely. "Not one of the two surgeons, clearly. But someone who saw you and me and then described me to Dandy. I'd start questioning the portering staff who were on duty the night the body was found, and the one we met yesterday. They're always willing to gossip, if offered enough beer."

Greig folds down the letter of complaint and reaches for an envelope. He has been maligned in the press, now he is being schooled on how to proceed with his investigation, and all on the back of getting very little sleep, as young Master Greig's teeth are coming in.

"Thank you, I shall bear it in mind," he says thinly. "Now, I must deal with the paperwork."

Stride shoots him a wry smile. "There's something I don't miss," he says. "Well, I just called by to commiserate. I'll leave you to get on, then. You know where to find me, should any developments occur."

The door closes. Greig unclenches his teeth and relaxes his shoulders. He has no intention of 'finding' Stride. After a few minutes have passed, he opens the door and calls for a constable, whom he instructs to go down to the London Hospital and collect the names of the relevant night staff together with the day porter who was on duty yesterday. That done, he picks up the first report from one of the night constables, which begins, as they always do: 'I was proceeding …'

Meanwhile, humming happily to himself, Stride makes his way down to the basement. His wife has put up a packet of ham sandwiches for his luncheon, much appreciated, and they will go down a treat after his chop and pint at Sally's. He unlocks the door, reaches for another box of reports and carries it across to the table where he has set up camp.

Of course, ex-Detective Inspector Stride tells himself, he has no intention of involving himself in Greig's current investigation. He has retired now. Nevertheless, it was his name on the initial letter, he reminds himself. And he was mentioned by name in that scurrilous Dandy's article. The game is afoot, he used to say to his colleagues, and maybe he still has a foot in the game.

****

It has been said that a rumour can spread faster than the truth can put on its boots. Thus, when Chief Inspector Greig returns to Scotland Yard from interviewing the hospital porters, discovering who it was who spoke to the press, and giving him an ear-bashing that he hopes he will never forget, he finds the waiting area full of anxious members of the public. Half are crowded into one area, half into the other, with a kind of no-man's land area separating them. He raises his eyebrows at the desk constable, who rolls his eyes, shrugs his shoulders, and shakes his head.

Greig moves into the empty space between the two groups. "Now then, my good people, what seems to be the matter here?" he says, in a brisk tone.

There is some dual-group shuffling. Eventually, a middle-aged man in a faded check cloth cap and paint-encrusted trousers is worked to the front of one of the groups. "Well, firstly, we ain't your good people, officer," he says sullenly. "We're here becoz we read about this deadly disease in the newspapers. And wot we wants to know is: wot is this disease? How do we know if we got it? And mostly, we wants to know wot are you a-going to do about it?"

Inwardly cursing, Greig folds his arms. "If you have any health worries ~ and I say 'if' ~ the place to take them is to your nearest doctor or to the hospital."

Cloth cap bridles. "We ain't a-going to no hospital. That's where they got all them dead bodies wot died of the disease."

Greig mentally notes the sudden growth in corpses.

"And anyway, they'll want paying. They always do. So, wot are you going to do about it, we wants to know?"

Mutterings of an affirmative nature rise from the other group. Greig looks from one lot of people to the other lot. "What on earth is going on? Why are you over here, and they are over there?"

A florid-faced woman with massive uncorsetted bosoms and wide hips steps forward and points at cloth cap. "We got here first. Then they came in. S'far as we know, they might have the deadly disease.

"You might have it, you mean," cloth cap retorts.

"No, you might have it," a voice shouts from the midst of the opposite group.

This is becoming like some gruesome pantomime. Greig holds up a hand for silence. "I can assure you that *none* of you probably have the deadly disease. Or any deadly disease. Now, I'm asking you all to go home. There is nothing to gain by being here. I am sure you have work to do. I strongly suggest that you go and get on with it, rather than wasting police time. And I urge you NOT to believe what you read in the newspapers."

There is a strong communal indrawing of breath at his words. Cloth cap produces a crumpled edition of the *Popular People's Gazette* from his pocket and points to it. "Are you saying the noospapers are *lyin'*?" he exclaims, his mouth gaping open at the outrageous suggestion.

"I'm saying that not everything you read is necessarily so," Greig counters. "Contrary to what the newspapers say, there are no singing mermaids in the Thames. Nor giant pigs in the Highgate sewers. And London is not in the grip of some deadly disease either. Just use your common sense, for goodness' sake! And now, please would you all leave. We have urgent criminal matters to deal with."

Greig moves towards the desk. Behind his back, the two groups, still regarding each other suspiciously, start to file out into the street. When the foyer is empty, apart from a few 'legitimate' individuals who have been waiting patiently on the Anxious Bench, he returns to his office.

This is a troubling development, he thinks. Because despite his confident assertion, there may be some truth behind the stories circulating in the public arena. So far, only one person has died. But if any more turn up ... Greig shudders. He is strongly tempted to go and talk matters over with Stride. But he resists the temptation. He is in charge now. He will deal with matters in his own way, which right now will be to sit tight and hope the death was a one-off event. He hasn't heard from the hospital, although experience has taught him that just because there's a silence it doesn't mean that nothing is going on.

****

Meanwhile Lucy Landseer, female private detective, has spent the morning in her Consulting Room writing a rather more extensive letter to the client whose errant husband she has tracked down. The letter informs the wife of the man's current address, his place of work, the public house in which he meets his mistress, and includes a bill for an investigation successfully completed.

After a sandwich luncheon, eaten at her desk, she moves on to her new case, which she has mentally named The Abandoned Infant Heiress. Lucy is fond of allocating names to her various investigations. She entered the detecting business on the back of a literary career that involved writing popular romantic short stories for various women's magazines, and an incredibly successful novel featuring Belle Batchelor (private investigator) and her faithful canine sidekick Harris.

Lucy has it in the back of her mind that one day, when she retires from her current occupation, she will rent an apartment somewhere warm ~ Italy comes to mind, where she will sit on a sunlit terrace overlooking an olive grove, with her typewriter, and compose stories about her experiences as a female detective. She certainly has enough material, although she would, of course, have to use fictitious names for the characters.

Now, she gathers her folder and writing material together and places them in her satchel. Then, leaving a note on her office door, she descends to street level and walks to the nearest omnibus stop. Her client might choose to travel by cab; she cannot afford such luxuries. After consulting her map a few times, she reaches the street where the Asylum for Female Orphans is located.

Lucy walks up and down the street, searching for some indication that she has found the place. To her surprise, there is none. On both sides of the street, she observes tall, well-appointed, three-storey houses, some with pots of geraniums on windowsills, some with elaborately-etched glass panels set in front doors. They give off an air of quiet respectability.

A couple of delivery carts pass her by. A nursemaid with a perambulator crosses the road. Lucy frowns, wishing the client had been a little more specific as to the exact house number. Still, it is not a long street, so if she starts at one end, she decides, and works her way along, she is bound to knock on the correct door eventually.

However, it takes more time to enact her plan successfully than she anticipates, for Lucy fails to factor in the novelty of a female detective arriving on the doorstep. As soon as her business card is handed over and taken to the mistress of the house, she is shown into the sitting room, and offered a cup of tea, which it would be impolite to refuse. She is then quizzed upon the nature of her occupation ~ her responses tempered with the need to be extremely circumspect. Family crimes and misdemeanours are then frankly divulged, and her opinion sought. It is amazing what goes on behind the respectable front doors of a quiet street in London! Hours pass, most interestingly, but Lucy is none the nearer to finding the asylum. Indeed, nobody has ever heard of an asylum for orphan girls in the street.

Eventually, just as she is giving up hope, she arrives at an end house set slightly back from the others. It has a shabby front door and the tiles leading up to it are cracked and broken. The windows are coated with grime and paint is flaking off the sills. Lucy pulls on the bell, hearing it echoing away into silence. After a long a pause, the door is opened, and Lucy finds herself looking down at a tiny, frail-looking person wearing a dark stuff gown of a previous vintage and an over-large lace cap. The person's thin cheeks are pale, her eyes lustreless. "Yes?" she whispers. "Who are you and what do you want?"

Lucy states her name and why she has called. She tries to work out whether she is addressing a child or a very small woman. She proffers her card. The person lifts it to within an inch of her eyes and studies it intently.

"But you have come too late. The children have all gone," she says, her voice etched with sorrow. "They left years ago. A wagon came in the early hours and all the furniture was put on it. Then the lady matron and the attendants took the children and the babies away." She hands back Lucy's card. "There is nobody here now but me, and Puss."

Lucy stares at her. "Where did they go?" she asks.

The child/woman shakes her head. "Away. To another place. A new better place. A man came and said the house wasn't suitable for them anymore."

"But you …?"

A small wry smile just lifts the corners of the mouth. "I wasn't wanted. I am too small. My legs, you see. There's something wrong with my legs. That's why I came here in the first place. And then they left, and they forgot about me. Once they remember, I will have to go to the workh'us I suppose."

Lucy is appalled. Over the creature's shoulder, she can just see a long, dark, unlit hallway, devoid of any furniture. How is this poor thing surviving? As if she reads her thoughts, the sole occupant of the empty asylum says, "There are some kind people who leave me little bits of food. And I have my cat. But I miss them, the children. Sometimes I hear them in the night, running along the corridor. Calling to each other. Laughing. There was an apple tree with a swing. A seesaw. I see them playing, out of the corner of my eye. 'Here we go up, up, up! Here we go down, down, down!' But by the time I turn my head, they've all gone. All the little ones have gone."

Her tiny face crumples. She peers up at Lucy, blinks a couple of times, then slowly retreats, closing the door. Lucy is left standing on the step, in the gathering twilight. She reaches into her bag and posts a few coins through the letterbox before turning to make her way back home. There is a lot to take in here, so she decides she will think it all out after some supper. One thing she is sure about: there has to be another way to track down the missing Broxton heiress. She just hasn't worked out what it is.

****

Meanwhile, in the basement of Scotland Yard, Stride checks his pocket watch and is surprised to see how many hours have passed. Down here it is like living in two worlds at once. He closes the case-file he has been working on; it is time to return to the present. Mrs Stride is a bit of a stickler about punctual attendance at the meal table.

Stride makes his way back up to street level, where the air smells unfresh, as if it has been breathed many times. A gas-light man with a long pole and a ladder is passing along the street. He, Stride, crosses Covent Garden piazza, heading for the coffee-stall holders on the corner. A quick mug of his favourite black treacly brew will set him up nicely for the walk home.

He has just paid for his drink, when he hears shuffling footsteps and hoarse breathing coming up behind him. Next thing, the smell of rotten teeth and unwashed body odour comes wafting into his nostrils. Stride turns. Standing much too close to him and breaching his personal space is Unfortunate Pegram, one of his many former informers. Stride hasn't seen him for a while ~ having stepped into the foreground to deliver their information, informers tended to blend hastily back into the background again.

"Evenin' Mr Stride, sir," Pegram mutters throatily. "Fort you'd retired from the detecting." He whips off his battered top hat, revealing a naked scalp covered in brown age-spots and bordered by a few whisps of matted hair. His eyes fix on the mug of hot coffee.

"Well, well, Mr Pegram," Stride says, taking a step back to get out of range of both the foul breath and the odours emanating from the moth-eaten overcoat and person within. "How are you faring nowadays?"

"Not so good, Mr Stride, sir. Gotta admit it." The eyes never leave the mug. "Might have a bit of information for you, though. 'Bout this man wot you lot are looking for."

"Man?" Stride queries.

"The one on the poster. Saw it down Marylebone p'lice office. Might know somefing about him. Might tell you wot I know. Might be worth a cuppa coffee an' a ham sangwidge?" he says, squinting up at Stride hopefully.

In all the years he used him, Stride never suspected Pegram could read. He summons up the requisite comestibles, then waits while Pegram wolfs down his supper. Eventually, when fingers have been run round the inside of the mug and sucked, the ex-informant burps contentedly and resumes.

"Where I doss down, at Ma Crocket's, over Whitechapel way, there's people coming and going all the time. Some pays for a bed; some goes to the night shelter and sleeps on the rope. Anyway, I fink the man ~ the one wot was on the poster, was there a week ago. Maybe it was him, maybe not. Off the Irish boat he was. Said he was going to work on a local building site. Spent a night sleeping on the rope."

"But you never saw him again?"

Pegram shakes his head. "People come and go all the time, like I said. But at least you got some useful information now, ain't yer?"

Stride tries to think how what he has been told will push the inquiry forward, comes to the conclusion that it is so vague that it probably won't, and deduces that he has just been scammed by the cunning old man for a free meal.

Meanwhile Pegram shuffles his feet, coughs moistly, spits a gob of something brown and repulsive on the ground and gives Stride a disgusting gummy grin. "Best be orf then, Mr Stride," he says. "Always here to help. Nice to see you back in ver saddle, as it were. 'Ope you catches your man." And he shambles off happily, leaving Stride to hurry home, where his dinner, which has been on the table for the past twenty minutes, awaits him. Along with his arms-folded, face-like-a-poker wife.

****

Violet Cully is also learning some useful information. Over the family supper table, she has shared what happened today to her and her friend May at the hands of the older pupil, Johanna Broxton. As she describes the older girl's appellation of the two of them as 'charity brats', Emily Cully exchanges a quick meaningful glance across the table with her husband.

Truth to tell, ever since Violet started at the new school, she has been waiting for something like this to happen. Waiting and dreading it at the same time, because it means she will have to explain how society works. Or rather, how some sections of it work. Tearing the mask off the cruel face of the class system and showing her bright young daughter that merit and brains count for very little in some people's opinion, and that there will always be snobs and rich people who will look down on her, breaks her loving heart.

Carefully, choosing her words and picking her way delicately across the verbal quicksand, Emily attempts to explain that money and birth and living in a big house make some people think they are more important than others. And that gives them the right, they believe, to behave in the way that this older girl did. Violet hears her out in silence. Then,

"Well, I do not believe a word of it!" she exclaims. "If that is what these people think, then they are quite wrong! Pa catches criminals. How important is that? And you make beautiful clothes. May's papa owns a hansom cab and a horse called Prince. Her mama comes from Italy. May has been to Italy many times and can speak the language. I do not see how any of this makes her or me inferior to some rich girl who arrives at school in a carriage. She doesn't own the carriage, does she? And I bet she can't speak Italian either!"

Jack Cully beams delightedly across the table at his daughter. "Well said young Vi! I have seen the insides of some of these rich houses, and met the people who live in them, and they are no better nor worse than we are. Some of them are decidedly much worse!"

"Really?" Violet sets down her spoon and leans towards him. "What do they do?"

Emily shoots him a warning look. There is a tacit agreement between them that Violet will be spared some of the nastier details of her husband's job. Sufficient unto the day. Jack Cully catches her eye and gives her a little nod of understanding.

"The main thing is, you do not sink to their level. Maybe you weren't born with a silver spoon in your mouth, but you know how to behave properly, which this girl, whoever her parents are, clearly does not. And never forget, you won your scholarship fair and square, and you have as much right to be in that school as she does, and nobody should ever call you a charity case."

The family finish their supper, then Violet and her younger sister help Emily to wash the pots, while Jack Cully settles down with the evening paper and gets his pipe going. Violet feels a certain tension in the air.

Things are not being said out loud, but they are still being communicated. After drying the last of the plates, she takes herself off to her small desk in the corner, where her homework is waiting. She called me a brat, she thinks, as she opens her school bag. But she will live to eat those words. And she, Violet, will live to see it happen.

****

It is a fine London morning. Milk carts rumble along the newly-swept streets. The first omnibuses prepare to take on their passengers ~ at this time of the morning it is mainly shop workers, and bank clerks, still heavy with sleep. Morning trains disgorge those passengers who have travelled into the city on a workmen's ticket. Barges and ferries ply their trade along the Thames, its water quicksilver in the pearl-coloured light.

Bakers, who've slaved over hot ovens all night, start piling their shop windows with newly baked bread as servants from the surrounding squares and terraces hurry out with their baskets to get the freshest rolls for their masters' breakfasts. Meanwhile, flower girls crowd round Covent Garden wholesalers, sorting and bunching their wares. Babylondon rises, shakes itself and prepares to greet another day, and another opportunity to make money.

And nowhere is that mindset more apparent than behind the high wooden facades erected under a lucrative contract from the Board of Works, to a firm of building contractors, who have been tasked with providing a small section of the brand new sewerage system that will take the human waste of millions of inhabitants and dispose of it downriver.

Nothing has ever been attempted on this scale in the history of the city, which has endured the unwholesome stench and presence of dung (human and animal) for hundreds of years. It is estimated that by mid-century there were cesspools beneath some 200,000 houses, with human waste frequently seeping through the wooden floors of the poorer households. Those who have migrated to the city over the centuries in the belief that the streets were paved with gold, find they had been grievously misled when their shoes come into contact with reality.

But today, behind a wooden hoarding bearing the message: ACKROYD & GUSKETT, CITY CONTRACTORS * DANGER OF DEATH * DEEP TRENCHES * KEEP OUT, all is unusually silent. Actually, it has been silent for the past few days, much to the bemusement of the local populace (those still left), who have endured the din of diggers, ringing of hammers, and shovelling of spades as the trench that will contain one section of the many sewers slowly advances southwards.

The change in this area has been swift and spectacular. Scarcely have the railway builders cleared away their debris than the sewer constructors have moved in. All around are scenes of desolation: familiar landmarks have disappeared, trees have been uprooted and houses teeter on the brink of destruction, with lines of staircases, and floors imprinted on their remaining walls.

There are two reasons for the current silence. One is a request from *The London Illustrated News* to be allowed to record the site, as they are currently mapping the disappearance of the city's historical past. As for the other reason ~ let us follow Edward Ackroyd, his bowler-hat, work suit and prominent stomach, as he alights from a hansom and cautiously approaches the works entrance.

Ackroyd produces a key from an inner pocket and works at the padlock securing the wooden door. It yields finally and he enters, taking the padlock with him. A necessary precaution. He crosses the site by means of a number of planks laid over the deep trench. Finally, he reaches the section that butts up against a very old stone wall, which might once have been part of the ancient city walls, centuries ago. He stops and looks down.

At the bottom of the trench, clearly outlined in the black ooze, are skulls, their greeny-white faces and eyeless sockets staring up at the unaccustomed sky. There are also shattered bones, and what looks like part of a small ribcage. And that's just the top layer. The young Irish navigator who was excavating this particular trench swears he struck more bodies … that was before climbing out and relaying what he found to the rest of the men, who immediately walked off the site, crossing themselves and saying the place was cursed and they wouldn't be coming back to work again.

This happened a few days ago. He has been unable to hire any more navigators, word having spread quickly amongst the Irish community. Whatever the truth of the matter, it has left Ackroyd & Guskett in a very awkward position. Their contract is for four months. If they don't finish laying the sewerage pipes, they won't get paid. And their reputation for getting the job done in time will be in shreds. They may never work in London again. As he stands contemplating the possible ruin of his business, he hears a voice calling his name. Ackroyd spins round, nearly toppling off the plank. He spies his partner, Anton Guskett, and behind him, three shabby, unshaved, unwashed, down-at-heel elderly individuals in ragged attire.

He hurries over. "What is going on?" he says, gesturing at the trio clustered behind Guskett. "Who are these men? Where on earth did you find them?"

Guskett plays with the ends of his dyed black mustachios. "Does it really matter, my friend? Let us just say, there are plenty of desperate folk who would do anything to keep from the poor house or the gaol. I promised them a fair day's wages for a fair day's work. Let us not inquire further. There is a cartload of sacks waiting in the road. The men will fill them, and we will dispose of the unfortunate contents ... elsewhere. All arranged. No questions asked. Money in hand is all these men care about," he pauses. "I have also ordered a barrel of beer to be delivered ... I think that will take the edge off any squeamishness, don't you?"

Ackroyd nods. Guskett is a 'fixer', and this is not the first time he has extracted the business from some problematic mire. Eyes on the bigger prize, Ackroyd reminds himself as he leads the way to the workmen's shed, where the shovels and wheelbarrows are stored. After each man has been equipped with the necessary tools, the sacks are brought in, and the shovelling and filling commences.

The elderly men make slow progress, and it is plain from their reactions that the task is being undertaken reluctantly. Ackroyd shouts and chivvies: the sooner the sacks are filled, and the men and the sacks disappear, the better. Then they can go about recruiting some proper navigators to finish the work. No more 'cursed ground'. The arrival of the cart bearing liquid refreshment brings the morning's labours to a summary halt.

However, when the men resume work, it soon becomes clear that the alcohol has not only dulled their senses but emboldened their behaviour. A skull, dug out of the green ooze, is roughly cleaned on a piece of sacking, then thrown into the air, where it becomes part of a lively and inappropriate game of 'catch'. Ackroyd attempts to restore discipline, but the motley crew are too inebriated to take much notice.

"'Ere, guv, catch a 'old a vis!" one dishevelled workman says, tossing the skull straight at him.

Ackroyd's natural reactions kick in and he catches the disgusting object. He is standing there, on the edge of the trench, the skull grasped in both hands, when the site door is flung open and a group of smartly dressed men enter. They are carrying tripods and cameras. Ackroyd gapes at them.

"*Illustrated London News,*" one of the men says, advancing towards him, with his card held in front of him. "We are here to map the area, record the historic buildings and report on the sewage excavations. You are expecting us? You received our letter?" His gaze travels down to Ackroyd's hands. "What on earth ...?"

The hapless contractor glances frantically around him: alas, there is no sign of Anton Guskett, fixer, anywhere. His partner has once again melted away into thin air, leaving him to deal with everything. Curse him, Ackroyd thinks, as he puts down the skull and advances towards the visitors with a ghastly grin on his face. Meanwhile, from behind him, a raucous chorus of very drunken old men break into an extremely scurrilous song, the words of which echo loud and clear across the site.

****

Ex-Detective Inspector Leo Stride finds himself caught upon the horns of a dilemma. Theoretically, he is no longer an employee of Her Majesty's Police Force (Detective Division). Therefore, he does not have the authority to investigate any current crimes or misdemeanours. That role has passed to Lachlan Greig ~ who is an excellent officer, efficient and much respected by the men working under him, Stride thinks, as his feet carry him towards Whitechapel.

Reflecting on his meeting with Unfortunate Pegram, he has fileted enough facts from it to make him decide to ask a few questions around the area where the dead man was last seen. After all, he reminds himself, it's not as if he is impinging upon Greig's territory: the sly old cadger approached him with the information. And if he discovers anything, he will immediately pass it on.

Stride passes by the London Hospital building and the Whitechapel Workhouse, which is just discharging its contingent of overnight sleepers, and strikes into the maze of little back-alleys and courts that stretch between Whitechapel church and Goodman's Fields. Here, the streets are crowded and mean, the houses small and ugly, huddled together as if for protection. Many of the front doors are open, showing kitchen fires ablaze and strange figures moving to and fro in the smoky air.

This was one of his first beats as a young constable, he recalls, as his feet tread upon cobbles that suddenly feel familiar. Memories flood back: dark alleyways swarming with the poor, the only light coming from a street corner where gin palaces flaunt their wares; tipsy women laughing brazenly as they tried to accost him; a mother and father with their two children, so worn away by hunger that they could barely stand upright.

A whole gallery of waifs and strays, rogues and vagabonds parade in front of Stride's imagination while in his mind he hears whistles, shouts, oaths, and growls. He steps over pools of black water and avoids piles of dust, human waste and rotting vegetables. Eventually, he finds an old man in corduroy breeches and dirty shirtsleeves sitting on a doorstep contentedly smoking a pipe, and asks for directions to 'Ma Crocket's'.

A few minutes' later, Stride enters one of the many low lodging houses. He discovers a small kitchen containing a couple of elderly women, and a child begrimed with dirt who is rolling upon the hearth. Rows of rags hang from a pulley over the kitchen fire. The women seem befuddled, even though it is still morning. Stride states the reason for his visit and is told that Ma has just 'shtepped out' for a penn'orth of gin.

Stride decides to stand on the broken step and await her arrival. Eventually, in the distance he spies a broad squat woman in a faded blue and white striped cotton dress, a black shawl wrapped round her shoulders and a formidable blue bonnet, with defunct avian adornment, clapped on her head. Her complexion errs on the crimson side, and her eyes, sunk into her skull like two currents in a bun, are dark and watchful. At her approach, various moochers and ruffians develop a sudden desire to move out of her way. She comes to a halt in front of Stride and looks up at him suspiciously.

"Now then, p'liceman, what d'you want here?"

Once again, as throughout his former career, Stride marvels at the ability of the general populace to identify any member of the constabulary, even if he isn't in uniform at the time. It's as if they walk through the world surrounded by some official aura.

"Are you Ma Crocker?"

"Who says so?"

Stride gestures over his shoulder towards the kitchen. The woman thrusts him aside and stalks into the house. A series of snarled exchanges ensue, culminating in the two women leaving the house at speed, The child sets up a dismal howling. There is the sound of a slap. The howling intensifies. Ma reappears.

"Now ven, you can state your business out 'ere." She gives him another hard look. "Waitaminnit, I knows you! Constable Leo Stride, innit?"

Stride acknowledges the appellation, explains that he is now a detective inspector. He decides to omit that he is currently retired, as it looks as if he is on the brink of making a discovery. "I am afraid I don't quite recall …" he says.

Ma folds her meaty arms under her saggy bosoms. "Well, ain't no surprise there. I 'ave gorn orff a bit over the years. Kate Bailey was my name back in the days. Bonny Kate the Music Hall Songbird. 'Walkin' Dahn Whitehall Way' ~ vat was my big number."

Memories come flooding back. A slender, dainty female, clad head to toe in sugar pink, pirouetting across the stage to great applause and wolf-whistles. In those far-off days, Stride and his companions used to frequent the Music Halls, either for the entertainment, or to help maintain law and order.

"You saved my sister Rosie from the Leman Street gang. I said back ven, I'd nivver forget it." Ma unfolds her arms and stands aside. "You come right in Mr Stride and makes yourself at 'ome. If'n I can help yer, I will. For Rosie's sake."

Suspending his disbelief at the contrast between Kate Bailey and the metamorphosed Ma Crocket, Stride follows Ma into the malodorous interior, where the child has curled itself up on the floor and fallen asleep.

"My grandson," Ma says, stirring it gently with a foot. "Little bugger, but his ma's doin' her best. No dad, o' course. Did a runner as soon as she started showin'. You won't see her, Mr Stride, she's sleeping off the night shift, if you take my meaning."

Stride lowers himself gingerly onto a 3-legged stool. Ma unhooks a big black kettle from over the fire. "Cuppa? I'd offer you summat in it, but I knows you don't take a drop when you're working, eh?"

Over a cup of tea so strong and well-brewed it could probably double as drain-cleaner, Stride tells Ma about the dead man. He omits the terrible nature of the death, focusing instead on the need to find out his identity so his family can be informed.

Twenty minutes later, Stride is heading back to Scotland Yard. He still doesn't know the identity of the young man, but he has a better idea of the nature of the casual work he was probably engaged upon. It is clear from what Ma Crocket told him that many Irish immigrants 'straight off the boats' slip past the government officials in Liverpool and take to the road, heading for London to work on the numerous building sites. Those that do not have good luck are caught by the port authorities and shipped straight back, to join their impoverished or landless families.

The young man in question had called in, having heard that there were other Irish navvies lodging with her, seeking a bed for the night. He had been directed elsewhere, as Ma was full up. That was all she knew. She had never seen him again. However, as a favour to Stride, she will mention his visit to the lodgers when they return from their labours. And if any of them remember the man, Ma will make sure he, Stride, will be the first to know.

Of course, Stride reminds himself, as he heads back to Scotland Yard, this is not his investigation as he no longer works as a detective, and anything useful he finds must be passed on to the new head of the Detective Division. He is merely acting as the go-between. The bridge, as he sees it. He is pretty sure Ma will be spreading the word of his arrival. Her lodgers will speak to her on the basis that she trusts him. Anyone else, Stride tells himself, would merely come up against a wall of silence. That is why it is up to him to pursue this interrogation as far as it can go.

A cacophony of church bells sounds the noonday hour. Time for his luncheon. Ex-Detective Inspector Stride decides to head for Sally's where he is sure his table will be waiting for him. And after putting the world to rights with mine host over a chop and a glass of ale, an afternoon of research awaits. If only he'd known retirement was this enjoyable, he might have considered it years ago.

****

Lucy Landseer is also indulging in some research. She has decided to consult the local parochial register, on the assumption that all foundling children would have to be formally named and registered. She has the date upon which the child had been deposited at the orphanage. It could be assumed that within a short time after her arrival, her name would be entered in the parish register.

So here she is, having dimpled and charmed her way into the office where the registers are kept, because if you have been born with feminine wiles, you might as well use them to your advantage. She is currently mounted on a high stool, where she is busily turning the pages of a bound copy of births from the year indicated by her client, looking for new-born baby girls where both the mother and father are unnamed.

Her search results in a couple of names that fit both the time, and the absence of parents. Now she has to discover where the former orphanage went once it closed. Lucy tries her charm offensive once more upon the officials in the registry, but alas, they are unable to help her.

However, Miss Lucy Landseer is not without resource or purpose. What many might think of as a setback is, in her eyes, merely a hurdle to be overcome. Lucy is an avid reader, and a great admirer of the works of Currer Bell, especially the novel Jane Eyre. Over a pot of tea and a slice of ginger cake in a local tearoom, she thinks about the early-life experiences of the eponymous heroine. Abandoned by her noxious family, Jane is placed in a 'Christian' school to receive a basic education prior to going out into the world to earn her living.

How likely is it, Lucy ponders, that these orphan girls would also be given a Christian education and upbringing to form their characters and disposition? How probable that the matron and her helpers attended Sunday worship? Their small charges would almost certainly be baptized and then taken to Sunday school when old enough to attend. Maybe the local minister called in to discuss their progress or deliver a sermon on the need for gratitude and humility? And she noticed that there is a church within convenient walking distance of the former orphanage. How fortunate.

Lucy is 'good' with the clergy, having been born a child of the manse. She knows how to accommodate herself to the various quirks and oddities of the profession without giving offence. She also knows exactly what the timetable of an Anglican minister looks like. Right now, he will be partaking of a midday meal, prepared by his housekeeper (or wife). After that, he'll retire to his study to work on his sermon for Sunday, before venturing out to visit the sick, and attend whatever committees need his presence.

Lucy has a brief window of opportunity between sermon and parish visits. She decides to seize it before it closes. Arriving at the church, she studies the noticeboard, which informs her that the minister is a Revd. Ichabod E. Sproule (Cantab.). The name has not been recently painted, a sign he has been minister in this church for a while. Hopefully within the existence of the Female Orphanage. She locates the manse: a gloomy building close to the cemetery and overshadowed by a large yew tree, marches boldly up the gravel pathway to the front door and pulls at the bell rope. After a few minutes, the door is opened by an elderly woman in a white apron and a lace morning cap. She regards Lucy hostily.

"I'm afraid we do not buy at the door, young woman," she says, curtly.

Lucy stifles a smile. This is exactly like her father's old housekeeper, who fended off parishioners and petitioners alike with a similarly frosty greeting.

"I am not here to sell anything," she says politely. "I am a private detective and have come to ask the minister a few questions on behalf of my client."

The housekeeper stares at her, animosity and curiosity playing across her features. Eventually curiosity wins, and Lucy is invited into a dark hallway, smelling of beeswax polish, conducted to an uncomfortable cane-bottomed chair and told to wait. The housekeeper takes her card and disappears, the words 'a lady detective ~ whatever next!' floating back behind her. Lucy folds her hands in her lap, the picture of meekness, mentally reliving her own childhood as she waits.

Do all manses smell of beeswax polish and cooked cabbage, she wonders? And do they all have the same paintings of men and women with haloes being killed in various unpleasant ways? St. Catherine on her wheel, St. Sebastian, naked to the waist, his chest covered with arrows dripping blood, St Ignatius being eaten by lions. She passed their portraits every night on her way up to her bedroom. No wonder she suffered from nightmares as a small child.

Eventually, the housekeeper reappears. "The minister says he can spare you five minutes only," she says stiffly. "He has an important committee meeting to attend."

"I am very grateful," Lucy replies sweetly, getting to her feet. She follows the woman to the door of a book-lined study, its dark crimson wallpaper, shoddy carpet, and sputtering fire that gives off no heat almost the replica of her father's study, where she and her brothers and sisters were forbidden to enter, lest they disturbed his contemplation of the scriptures.

"Here's the lady detective, sir," the housekeeper announces in a tone dripping with disapproval.

Revd. Ichabod E. Sproule is a tall man with dark hair streaked with grey at the temples. He has very thick black brows, and very bushy side whiskers. Clad in a black suit, he is standing on a rug in front of the inadequate fire. Lucy tries hard not to think of Mr. Brocklehurst, but fails.

"Good afternoon, Miss ... Landseer," he says, his eyes flicking down to her card. "I confess I am at a loss to understand the purpose of your visit. I am afraid you will find no crimes nor misdemeanours here. We are a law-abiding house. Christian people. Perhaps you can enlighten me?"

Noticing that she has not been invited to sit down, and interpreting it correctly, Lucy launches into her explanation. The minister hears her out. Then,

"A young woman who indulged her carnal appetite. A child born out of holy wedlock. I see. Abandoned at the Orphanage. I understand. You are quite correct,

Miss Landseer. The illegitimate children were brought to the church for the ceremony of baptism. It was my Christian duty to admit them into God's kingdom. And again, some did attend Sabbath school. As for the current orphanage, I believe I have a letter from the matron informing me of the new location, but I will have to go through my correspondence, which might take some time. I will write to you once I have found it."

Lucy attempts to explain the urgency of the matter, but the minister holds up a large white be-ringed hand. "Let me stop you right there, Miss Landseer. The parent of this abandoned child ~ your 'client' as you call her ~ has waited many years to reclaim her, is that not so? Then I am sure she can wait a bit longer, can she not?"

Lucy clamps her lips tightly together. She is entirely in his disapproving hands. So she merely thanks him politely, and is shown back out by the housekeeper, her back stiff with stony rectitude. It is only later, when writing up her notes for Miss Broxton and her sister, that she allows herself to express her anger, which takes the form of hurling an empty inkpot at the wall and uttering the words 'sanctimonious' and 'brute' several times.

****

We left Stride heading for a hot luncheon, to be followed by an afternoon of research for his upcoming memoirs (title still to be decided, but *'The Curious Casebook of a London Detective'* is the current favourite). As he passes through the doors leading into Scotland Yard, he spies Lachlan Greig in deep conversation with a man he recognises as the young surgeon they encountered at the London Hospital. Both wear worried expressions. Stride approaches.

"Ah, detective," the surgeon says. "I was just asking your colleague where you might be found."

Stride catches the edge of Greig's glance and reads it. "I am retired, so I am no longer working as a detective," he says hastily. "I am here on a personal matter only."

"Nevertheless," the surgeon persists, "Sir Charles wished me to speak to you." He pauses. "There's been another death," he says, lowering his voice. "One of the porters. The man who originally took in the body. They found him in his room ~ some of the men live on the hospital premises. He hadn't been seen since he went off duty." His voice falters. "He was an old man; he'd worked for the hospital for many years. I knew him, to say 'good day' to only. He must've known what was coming and deliberately shut himself away. I can hardly bear to think about his final hours."

Stride decides to wait for Greig to respond. A long minute passes before he does. "I am sure we are both extremely sorry to hear this. Very sorry indeed. But what do you expect us to do? At your request we have kept this very low key. We have not spoken to the newspapers ~ unlike your own staff, who had to be reprimanded for giving an interview to one of the lowest reporters of the fifth estate. As I see it, we either make a public announcement that at least two cases of plague have occurred in the city, resulting in two deaths, and as a consequence risk the whole of London going into complete panic, or we pursue our inquiries with stealth, speed, and persistence. Which, exactly, do you wish us to do?"

The surgeon looks away, shifting awkwardly from one foot to the other. "We are one of the most admirably conducted institutions in the whole of

England, you see," he says. "We have a brand-new wing being built. Our board consists of a royal personage as well as captains of industry. We have ten physicians, and surgeons, thirty sisters, and over two hundred nurses. We simply cannot let our hospital governors and sponsors know of this matter. The most important thing is to maintain the spotless reputation of the hospital."

Greig's expression is now unreadable. Except to Stride, who is reading him loud and clear.

"We are relying on your discretion, detective," the surgeon continues, when the silence between the three men becomes so dense it could be cut and served in slices. "Yes. That is what we are going to do. We want a speedy resolution. We hope that it will be the case. Now, I expect you have police business to pursue. I have a full slate of operations, so I will bid you both good day."

Greig and Stride watch him walk across the foyer and disappear out into the teeming street.

"I suppose the deaths of a young Irish navigator and an elderly hospital porter are not especially important, in the great scheme of things," Stride says drily. "Our good surgeon had better hope that nobody more significant goes down with it. That might create problems that would be much harder to brush under the carpet, whatever the spotless reputation of the London Hospital."

****

Brushing things under carpets ~ or rather, hiding them under tarpaulins is exactly what Edward Ackroyd has been doing. Having invited *The Illustrated London News* journalists to 'step outside and give me a half-hour to deal with matters here', he has ushered them off the site. As soon as the door closed on them, Ackroyd angrily rounds up and dismisses his drunken labourers, saying they would get their money when they were sober enough to come back for it (i.e. never). Then, hauling a tarpaulin out of the shed, he has hastily thrown it over the trench and secured it with bricks and the barrows. Just as he finishes, his partner, Anton Guskett, cigar in one hand, re-appears.

"I say old chap, what's going on? Just met our men in the street, roiling drunk. Have they finished the job already?"

Ackroyd regards him sourly. Memories of other sites, other problems and the absence of Guskett rise up to taunt him. Whenever there is a difficulty, somehow his partner is never on hand to deal with it.

"Where've you been?" he growls crossly. "I've had to deal with your workmen ~ though 'work' is hardly the word I'd use. And we have some newspaper johnnies about to descend to 'survey the site'. They wrote to us. I don't recall ever seeing a letter. One way and another, I could've done with you here."

Anton Guskett shrugs, blows a smoke ring. "I'm sure you have dealt with things. Meanwhile, I have been reeling in our new investor. Met him at my club. Been wining and dining him for a while, softening him up. He's prepared to put a tidy sum our way. Which we will need if we are going to bid for the next round of contracts. Which we are. I've heard on the old grapevine that there's a site over by the embankment coming up for development. The Board of Works is inviting tenders for it. We would be up against some of the big boys, but if we can get this job finished to time, and we can show we have the funds in the bank, that would be to our advantage."

Ackroyd pulls a face. Somehow, Guskett always has a valid reason for being elsewhere. Though in this case, it seems he was doing something for the company, as opposed to something for himself. "Well, the newspaper men will be along in a few minutes," he says, grudgingly. "You're better at dealing with these sorts of people than I am. I think they just want to make some drawings and take photographs. Not that there's anything to see. I advise you do not let them linger by that tarpaulin, though. The sacks are underneath it."

Guskett taps the side of his long nose with a nicotine-stained index finger. "Receiving your message, old man. And I think this is them arriving now. Tell you what, you go and grab yourself a sandwich and a glass of something, and I'll turn on the old charm. Soon get rid of them."

"And the sacks?"

"Not a problem. There's always men willing to do any dirty job, for a price. By tomorrow, the sacks will have gone. Leave it to me. Have I ever let you down? Now, you toddle off. Give it a couple of hours, then we can go and meet the new investor. I think you'll like him. You'll like his money even more."

Guskett claps Ackroyd genially on the shoulder. "Bear up, old chap. Nothing is going to go wrong." He advances upon the group from *The Illustrated London News*, his hand outstretched, a broad smile of welcome plastered on his face. "Morning, gentlemen," he beams. "Sorry about that little bit of business earlier on. You just can't find the workers nowadays, can you? My partner has got it all dealt with. Now, where do you want to begin?"

Leaving Anton Guskett to usher the journalists and their photographer onto the site, Ackroyd slips out of the site door and makes his way down the street. It is almost as if the site really is cursed, he thinks wearily.

Certainly, he has never encountered anything like this before, in all his years of building and construction.

****

Jasper Broxton, entrepreneur, conducts his business affairs from the first floor of a smart, modern office in the city. He conducts his other affair from a small villa in St John's Wood. This afternoon he is in his office, busily dictating letters to Wilberforce, his clerk.

"… And as a valued client of Broxton Business Investment & Financial Services, I am writing to offer you, at the earliest opportunity, the chance to invest in this construction company, who have already secured numerous commercial government contracts and expect to obtain many more, thus incrementally increasing their profits and that of their fortunate shareholders. It is an opportunity not to be missed and is only being offered to selected clients of mine, on a first come basis. I await your speedy response, respectfully yours, etc. etc." He waves a dismissive hand. "See that a copy is sent to everybody on the list by close of today."

As soon as his clerk has left, Broxton gets out his pocketbook, in which he has inscribed a list of certain members of his club. He intends to write each a personal letter inviting them to contribute to his upcoming venture. These are men he's wined and dined, flattered, and fawned over for the past few months. He'd selected them for their personal vanity as well as their wealth (the two frequently go hand in hand). With these individuals, he intends to pursue a different tack though, reminding them, casually, that he is on the brink of inheriting substantial properties and a small fortune when his childless cousin passes away.

Broxton's plan is to use some of the money from his club acquaintances to pay off his creditors. Then, in time, he will use some of the money from his clients to pay them back. A sum will also be invested in the construction company ~ enough to keep the two owners indebted to him. If, as the flashy one promised, they were on the brink of a major contract, he intends to make sure he has a large slice of profit pie ~ on the basis that he'd threaten to withdraw his funds if he didn't. Money with menace is always the best leverage.

And of course, even if all his schemes went belly-up, there is always the Broxton inheritance, which is coming nearer every day that his sickly cousin draws breath. His wife Avice has managed to place a servant in Margaret Broxton's London house, and her letters are keeping them abreast of progress on that front. Broxton reaches for his cheque book and writes out a cheque for Shedleigh's school fees, post-dated. It wouldn't do to have the boy sent home. An event like that could become public and might cause some people of a nervous disposition to rethink their investments. Besides, it will stop Avice from nagging at him, something in which she is rapidly becoming an expert.

Broxton hauls a gold-chained watch up from his waistcoat pocket. He has just time to consume a light luncheon before his next meeting. Then he must visit his lawyer to get the necessary documents drawn up, and see if the lawyer has had a reply from his cousin to his latest letter. He doubts it ~ she seems to be adopting a policy of silence. No problem. It is only a matter of time, and then the entire Broxton estate: farm, manor house, lands, and money, will pass by default into his hands.

****

It is late afternoon, and it is raining. Not a gentle spring rain though, this is full-on rain with the volume turned up. Rain overflows gutters and splashes onto greasy pavements. Rain splatters on shop windows, cascades off umbrellas as people dodge and weave along footways. Carts and carriages stop and start. Everything is blurred. The whole city moves like slightly faulty clockwork.

Look more closely: two bedraggled small figures are making their way through the slanting grey rain. They carry bookbags; their hats are shapeless; their tunics cling to their wet legs. It is the end of the school day and Violet Cully and her friend May Higgins are returning to their respective homes. They had waited for the omnibus, but when it arrived, it was almost full, and before they could board, they were pushed aside by several women with shopping. Now they are walking between stops, getting wetter by the second.

"Do you think this is what the Flood was like?" May shouts.

"If you take away the traffic and the houses, I think so," Violet replies.

Suddenly May points, "There's an omnibus ~ if we run, we might get on it!"

Both girls set off at a sprint. They almost reach the bus stop when a closed carriage suddenly veers towards them, sending a wall of filthy water that engulfs them both. Shocked, the two girls stare after the rapidly disappearing vehicle.

"Did you see who it was?" May gasps, wiping water out of her eyes.

Violet nods grimly. "I bet she got the driver to do that deliberately," she says. "Come on, May, let's get out of the rain for a bit. I know somewhere we can go, and I have enough money for a hot drink. We can share it and plot our next move. And we'll add that soaking to our tally."

Violet squelches her way along the High Street until she turns abruptly off the main thoroughfare. After a short distance, she enters a small side street. Halfway down, she stops outside a tea-room, its windows steamed up on the inside, rain dripping down the glass. A sign proclaims that it is called the Lily Lounge. Violet pushes open the door, and they enter. The tea-room is full of customers enjoying plates of cakes while waiting for the rain to subside. Uniformed waitresses weave between tables, carrying trays piled with plates and cups.

"Vi, we oughtn't to have come in here," May whispers, as the two girls stand on the threshold, dripping water from their hats onto the polished floor. "It's a smart place."

But Violet takes her arm and steers her over to the counter. "Is Mrs Marks here?" she asks one of the white-aproned waitresses. On being informed that Mrs Marks is in the kitchen downstairs, Violet says, "Then please can you go and tell her that Violet Cully and a friend have just come in."

The waitress regards her sceptically, but Violet holds her gaze until she mutters something and leaves the room. A few minutes and a puddle later, the door to the back of the tea-room is opened and a tall, imposing, grey-haired woman wearing black enters. At her appearance, the waitresses behind the counter stand up a little straighter and busy themselves with various tasks.

"Violet Cully!" the lady exclaims, hurrying over. "Goodness me. It is you. But you have grown so tall! And you are soaked to the skin!"

Violet explains about the rain, the lack of omnibuses and the soaking at the hands of the passing carriage.

"You poor dear lambs," Lilith says. "Come, let us all go into the back kitchen. It is nice and warm there and you can dry off in front of the oven. I expect you'd like a cup of tea and some seed cake, wouldn't you?"

Both girls brighten up at the kind offer, and a short while later, their outer garments steaming on a wooden clothes rail, their shoes propped upon the fender, they sip their tea, munch their cake, and enlighten Mrs Marks about the feud with Johanna Broxton and their plans to get their own back on her. And Lilith laughs and says she is glad she isn't Johanna, for the two of them are clearly a force to be reckoned with. After which, the rain having eased, and their clothes dried sufficiently, she fills a box with cakes for Violet's parents and finds a hansom to take them both home.

"No, no, I shall always be in debt to your papa and your mama," she says, waving away Violet's profuse thank-yous. "Any time you girls are caught in the rain, or the snow, or need somewhere to do your plotting, there will always be a pot of tea and a slice of cake waiting," she continues, as she instructs and pays the cabby, and then bids them goodbye.

The cab drops the two girls at their respective homes, where Emily Cully is relieved to see Violet arrive safe and dry, having worried about how her daughter has fared in the torrential downpour. Later, over supper, Violet asks about the 'debt' that Lilith mentioned as she put them into the cab, and in return, Emily tells her about the daughter Lilith thought had died, but in reality had been taken and given to a rich family to bring up as their own. She goes on to describe how Jack Cully tracked down the daughter, who had run away from her rich family, realised who she was in reality, and persuaded her to return to London to meet her real mother.

"You were a tiny girl, and I was a complete stranger to Mrs Marks, when we went to her tearoom for the first time," Emily says. "I was carrying the letter from your papa saying that her daughter had been found. And later, your papa and Mr Stride, who was his boss in those days, brought the girl ~ well, she was really a young woman by the time they found her, back to the café. It was a wonderful thing that happened. And that's why Mrs Marks always sends us a lovely Christmas cake every year. It's her way of saying thank you."

Violet finishes her supper in thoughtful silence, then migrates to her desk to begin her homework. But when Cully finally returns from Scotland Yard, she watches him covertly from her study corner. Previously, she'd thought he only chased after and arrested criminals. Now she has learned something new about what he does all day. And what she has learned is exactly like something out of a fairytale. Violet Cully eyes her young sister thoughtfully, as her imagination starts firing on all cylinders. As soon as she has completed her homework, she intends to start writing a drama based on what she has been told by her mother. There might even be a part for the family cat ~ if it can be persuaded to participate.

****

Sadly, Edward Ackroyd's life does not resemble any fairytale. Here he is, selecting his breakfast viands from the laden buffet at his hotel, for Ackroyd does not live in London, preferring the cleaner air of the cathedral city of St Albans. When working on a site in his capacity as overseer he prefers to stay at the Charing Cross Hotel in the Strand, returning to hearth and home by train at the weekend. Ackroyd piles his plate with kedgeree, bacon, a couple of fried eggs, hooks a rack of toast and finds a secluded corner to consume his food. He is not one of those gregarious individuals who enjoy conversing at breakfast.

A waiter glides silently over bringing a silver coffee pot, sugar bowl and milk jug on a tray. The staff know the likes and dislikes of their regular clientele. Ackroyd sugars the coffee and dips a toast triangle into the egg yolk. He is a formidable trencherman, claiming that working in the open air justifies the size of his meals. The irony that he never does an actual hands-turn, and that the men labouring for him are lucky if they get a slice of bread and a mug of cold tea has never entered his thinking.

It is a shock, therefore, when the double doors to the breakfast room are abruptly thrust open and a familiar figure stands on the threshold. Ackroyd's heart sinks. He attempts to hide behind a square of toast. To no avail. The figure bounds across the room, pulling out the chair on the other side of his secluded little table. Ackroyd sighs. Now what?

"Morning, old man," Anton Guskett says. He slaps a copy of *The Illustrated London News* on the table, almost upsetting the cup of coffee. "Read this: we are in big, big trouble."

Ackroyd follows the pointing finger: *Archaeology of the Month*, he reads. Then: '*Excavation for a new sewer uncovers original City walls*'. The heading is above an extremely well-drawn and accurate map of the whole construction site. Alongside it are a couple of photographs that clearly show the trench, covered by a tarpaulin. The article goes on to discuss the historical importance of the 'find', along with a brief history of Medieval London. His face falls as the significance of what he is reading hits him.

"Read the final paragraph," Guskett says urgently. "Then you'll see what I mean."

Ackroyd skims down to the end of the article: *'Before this site is completely covered in, and the precious historical remains lost for ever, we recommend readers to visit and see for themselves a rare section of the ancient stone walls that kept the old City safe. It is well worth a trip.'* He looks up, his face ashen. "But we simply cannot have members of the public traipsing all over the site. It is not safe."

"Indeed not," Guskett says. "And that area in particular."

"You have got rid of the sacks, haven't you?" Ackroyd queries.

There is an awkward pause.

"Haven't you?" he asks.

Guskett twirls the ends of his moustaches. "You see, old man, it's like this: I tried. Damn hard. But word has got round, and nobody will touch it. I was told one of the bog-trotters mysteriously disappeared after working on the site and the story is that he was taken away by the spirits of the dead as a punishment for disturbing them. Utter piffle and balderdash. But rumours spread amongst these people."

"So, are you saying that the sacks are still there under the tarpaulin?" Ackroyd gasps, feeling his breakfast settling like lead in his stomach.

Guskett looks off. "Might have to shift them ourselves at the end of the day, I'm afraid. Look, old man, you finish up here. I'll go down to the site and fend off any unwelcome visitors. I'll tell them we are making the site safe by building a viewing platform, and it will be open in a day or so. How does that sound?"

"And the sacks?"

"We can move them tonight, under cover of darkness."

"We?" Ackroyd looks horrified.

"I'll see if I can round up a couple of men to help ... but remember, the fewer who know about the bones, the more chance we have of luring labourers back. These people may be simple, but they have long memories. Our best hope is to clear the site completely, then hire fresh workers from Liverpool ~ straight off the boat. I have already sent O'Connor to round some up."

Ackroyd thinks about this for a while. "Have you ever wondered who these people were?" he asks eventually. "And why their bodies were just dumped in a pit outside the walls and not buried in a churchyard?"

Guskett shrugs. "I really don't care, old man. The important thing is not who they were, but where they are going. Which is to the bottom of the river, with a load of bricks to make sure they never resurface." He rises, gathers up the newspaper. "Enjoy the rest of your breakfast. No hurry. I'll fend everyone off until you arrive."

And he is gone.

Ackroyd sits on, staring gloomily at his plate of congealing egg and cold bacon, his appetite now completely vanished. His breakfast unfinished, he returns to his room to complete his morning routine. Eventually, hatted, gloved, and dismayed, he leaves the hotel and sets off through the noisy, smelly city, mentally cursing the journal that has taken it upon itself to turn his building site into a tourist attraction. Was it not bad enough that Murray's Handbook of Modern London contained a section on 'metropolitan improvements' which had dogged their progress on a previous site? Ackroyd recalls with a shudder the groups of tourists, each with their edition of the handbook, turning up at regular intervals to view 'the entire street architecture' ~ which included the drains his company was laying down. He was horrified to discover there was actually a section in the handbook devoted to 'Main Drainage'.

What is wrong with modern tourists, he wonders? They have the seaside, the whole of the continent, even Scotland, yet they prefer to stand gawping at a building site, while getting in the way. Which is exactly what he encounters when he approaches the sewer excavations. Although in this case, the crowd is gawping at a notice affixed to the entrance, which informs them that the site is currently closed for viewing while various safety measures are put in place, but visitors will be welcomed from 10.30am tomorrow.

Ackroyd spots several recognisable spectators: the elderly gentleman in the frock coat, his top hat slightly taller than current fashion dictates. He has a silver-topped walking stick, with which he is pointing out the imaginary features on the other side of the high wooden fence to the same young lady who was with him last time, her chestnut curls hidden under a neat bonnet. Ackroyd presumes she is his ward. Also in the group are the three serious men in shabby suits who always carry notebooks. He has decided they are academics. They bicker a lot. The rest are unknown to him, being a motley collection of London citizenry and visitors. The ubiquitous un-owned small brown dog is also in attendance, sniffing round the base of the fence, its tongue lolling.

Head down, Ackroyd sidles past them and unlocks the padlock. Ignoring the pleas for admittance, he slides through the door, firmly padlocking it on the other side. He waits until the knocking and calling has subsided, then, his heart beating uncomfortably in his chest, he picks his way across the various plank bridges to the far side of the site, where the 'ancient wall' rises by the tarpaulin-covered trench.

Lifting the tarpaulin, Ackroyd observes that the trench has become waterlogged after the recent rain. The sacks are stained and oozing. There are still some bones protruding from the earth underneath. He attempts to lift one of the sacks but has to give up. It will be a two-man job to manoeuvre them into the barrows, shovel up the remaining bones, and then to push the barrows through the darkened streets to the nearest river access. And what if they get stopped by a night constable? How will they explain the gruesome contents? And the whole ghastly business will have to be done and dusted tonight, or they will lose the contract and their names will be on the front pages of every newspaper and their reputation will be dragged through the court of public opinion.

Uttering a little moan, Ackroyd sinks to the muddy ground and covers his face with his hands. When his father died and he took over Ackroyd & Son Construction Company, in the halcyon days before he went into partnership with Anton Guskett and allowed himself to be lured to London on promises of riches untold, he never envisaged anything like this happening.

All at once, something moves, just on the edge of his eyeline. He stares down fearfully, his mouth suddenly dry, his breath catching in his throat. A black cat crosses in front of him, carrying a dead rat in its mouth. A symbol? A sign of bad luck? Get a grip for God's sake, he tells himself. The dead are dead. They aren't going to come back. Ever. Tomorrow, we will begin work again with a fresh crew and everything will go as planned.

****

The deaths of Kings and Queens are marked by weeks of national mourning, black-bordered newspapers, flags flown at half-mast and a state funeral with a draped coffin born on a gun-carriage, surrounded by soldiers in full dress uniform playing solemn funeral music.

The deaths of the rich are marked by black bows on front doors, notices in the personal columns of the better newspapers, visits to Robinson's mourning department, and an internment in the family vault, preferably on the family estate, or if not, in some fashionable venue like Highgate or Kensal Green.

The deaths of the homeless and derelict are rarely noticed or marked by anybody. So, when the bodies of three elderly derelict vagrants, soaked to the skin and smelling strongly of drink, lie huddled together in the undergrowth on a patch of waste ground, the man walking by with his two spaniel dogs doesn't notice them at all.

The dogs, however, show decidedly more interest. They approach the bodies and sniff them. They whine uneasily. One paws at a ragged coat, which disintegrates, revealing a grey-skinned arm, with blackened finger-ends and a black egg-like swelling in the armpit. They start to bark. At which point, the man registers that his pets have found something, and wanders over to see what it is.

The dogs' owner is an Oxford antiquary, philosopher and academic. He is writing a treatise on London in the reign of Charles the Second ~ his particular area of interest, which means he is one of the few non-medical people to recognise what he is seeing. For several minutes he stares down, a frown furrowing his academic brow. He pokes at the bodies with his stick. Then, muttering something about the inaccuracy of Defoe, he rounds up the spaniels (Charles and Henrietta) and sets off at a brisk pace in the direction of his lodgings. In a few hours' time, he will be delivering a lecture to the Royal Society. This discovery will now form part of it.

And here he is. Professor Aubrey Summerton, the Oxford antiquary and philosopher stands behind a podium on a raised dais in a private room, facing an audience of his fellow academics, all allegedly eager to hear his lecture on 'The Misrepresentation in Daniel Defoe and other authors of various Aspects of Mid-to-Late Stuart London'. The evening has begun well, with a nice meal, at which he was placed next to Lord Henry St. John Meakin, the chairman of the London Historical Antiquarian Society. He has also met the editor of *The Illustrated London News*, who is here with some of his journalists. The rest of the audience consists of elderly, erudite, male academics who, while they wait for the main speaker, are engaged in their favourite pastime: quibbling over small footnotes and marginalia. And at the back sit ordinary members of the public ~ for these lectures are open for all to attend.

Replete and ready, Summerton spends a few seconds fussing with his notes, then looks up. The room quietens. Eyes are turned towards the diminutive grey-bearded figure in his old-fashioned frock coat and high white stock. Summerton has always, from his public school years, conveyed in his physical appearance and demeanour, the impression of someone from a much earlier century.

He begins with some jocular references to the state of the contemporary city, allying them subtly to the century he is about to speak on. He then launches into his main argument, citing passages from writers of the time that disagree or contradict each other and laying over them the sheen of his own interpretation. In the course of his lecture, he manages to get in a passing reference to some dead bodies he saw earlier, derelicts, whose condition he observed, and whose appearance belies the descriptions of plague in the work of both Defoe and various other contemporary writers. At the end of his lecture, which is greeted with polite applause, he fields questions from the audience, then after a vote of thanks, he is ushered off the stage by Lord Meakin.

As Summerton is gathering his things together, feeling pleased with the way his lecture was received, he is approached from the back of the hall by a tall man in his late thirties. He is broad shouldered, with chestnut coloured hair, and an expression that seems to denote he does not tolerate fools gladly. Summerton bestows upon him the benign smile that he always gives to non-academics that he meets. It is not their fault that they have not acceded to the higher realms of academe.

"Thank you for your very illuminating lecture, professor," the man begins.

Summerton nods his acceptance of the compliment. In the case of members of the general public, to which this man clearly belongs, he adopts an air of humoured tolerance. After all, not everybody is fortunate enough to reach his level of intellectual superiority.

The man produces his card. "I am Chief Inspector Lachlan Greig, head of the city's Detective Division," he says. "I'd be grateful if you would accompany me to Scotland Yard. I wish to ascertain from you exactly where you discovered these dead men. And more importantly, I would like to know the reason why you failed to report what you found to the police authorities."

****

Darkness falls. The gas lamps are lit, and the flames burn, blurring the boundaries between the real and imagined worlds. By daylight, London is a city of commerce and movement, by night, a world of danger and disorder. *Carpe noctem.* London at night presents a parallel world, a slippage between the strange and the familiar. Strange figures appear, phantoms arrayed in satin and lace flit past, intent on pursuing pleasure. The air is rent by screams and raucous voices. Weird shuddering echoes distort and confuse the night walker, while the street lamps flicker like corpse-candles.

Look more closely. Two men, overcoated, hatted, gloved. Not, from their gait, drunk. Not, from their location, out on a spree. Not, from the wheelbarrows they are pushing, having a fun night. Not from their furtive demeanour, engaged in anything legal. So thinks the young lady who is on her way to the Dog & Diamond for a brief glass of something restorative to get her through the rest of her night shift, because in her line of work, it is hard hanging about on street corners waiting for customers to pass by and anyway, at the moment, her bed is being used by someone else in the same profession.

The young lady is intrigued, (her name is Temperance, which is a hard name to live up to, so she doesn't). Also, there are rumours circulating of a gang who have moved into the area and are helping themselves to people's property and carting it off to sell south of the river ~ a heathen godless place where people eke out a miserable existence in squalor and shame, and now with stolen furniture. So, eschewing the drink temporarily, and adopting the role of upstanding (as opposed to downlying) citizen, albeit temporarily, she starts following the barrow boys, always keeping to the shadows, ducking into doorways and convenient alleys every time they pause for a breather.

She follows them along Union Street, then Lambeth Street, only pausing when they reach Dock Street, and their destination becomes clear. Then, she retraces her steps, stopping off at the public house for that welcome drink. She is just finishing the last of her restorative beverage and eyeing the clientele in the public bar with a view to finding a bit of business ~ she is an opportunist by nature, when the two men she has been shadowing enter the bar.

Temperance picks up her almost empty glass and sidles nonchalantly towards the pair, watching as they order some drinks and carry them to a secluded booth. They lean across the table, speaking in low voices so as not to be heard by customers, but after a beating from a particularly violent client, Temperance is slightly deaf and is quite used to lip-reading. As she follows the conversation, several things puzzle her. These men are not the usual sort of rough and ready types who are to be found in a public house like this. They are clearly of a better class. She can tell by the way they speak. Which in itself means they must be very much up to no good.

She listens for a while. One is clearly jittery. Scared of something. The other one is reassuring. Sacks. Sacks. The jittery one drains his pot as if he has a thirst on him. Then he gets up. She turns her head, pretends to be fascinated by the smoke-stained wall. He hurries past her, the fear coming off him like smoke. She follows him out, watches him pick up one of the wheelbarrows and set off down the road, running as if the devil is after him. Strange, she thinks, filing it somewhere at the back of her mind. She returns to her beat. The night is waning, but if she is lucky, there are still a few hours of work left.

Her sentiments are shared by Constable Timothy ('Tibbs') Cook, who is on night patrol in the area. He has recently joined the Metropolitan Police, having finally reached the requisite height, and passed the examination. He is proud to be wearing the uniform, with its bright buttons, stout belt, whistle, and truncheon. He polishes the buttons every evening before retiring to his bed in the station house dormitory. He has been on duty since 10 o'clock, looking for miscreants and felons. Every now and then, he meets up with two other constables for a quiet smoke in a doorway. He is so new, Constable Cook, that he hasn't yet mastered the art of 'proceeding' ~ the slow pace of walking a beat that is germane to all police officers. Cook still marches along as if he was in the army and on his way to the battlefield.

Let us pause awhile to consider the role of the lowly Metropolitan Police constable. The total length of the streets and roads regularly patrolled is not less than 6,708 miles. It is divided into 921 day-beats and 3,136 night-beats ~ such as the one currently being patrolled by Constable Cook. The average length of the day-beats is seven and a half miles; the night-beats a little over 2 miles. The night constables go on duty at 10 o'clock in the evening and remain until 6 o'clock in the morning, and they are charged with, amongst other duties, looking after beggars, street tramps and nuisances, checking letterboxes and street lamps, seizing stray dogs and taking charge of lost children. They are also charged with observing *the conduct of any suspicious person/s hanging about a house and to take notice of anyone carrying away parcels or bundles at unseasonable hours under suspicious circumstances* (***General Regulations, Instructions, and Orders***).

Constable Cook is sure he heard the faint faraway sound of splashing, coming from the dock area. Not the sound of a rope being cast off, he decides. More like something falling into the water. Or somebody? Perhaps they are trying to drown someone? Whatever it is, it's definitely suspicious, and it is his bounden duty as a keeper of the peace to investigate. So, just as the two barrow boys have dumped their last load of sacks into the water and are vacating the scene as fast as their exhausted legs will carry them, the constable makes his way towards the docks. At a brisk march.

Reaching the jetty, Cook peers down into the dark river. The water ripples gently, reflecting back lights on the ships' mastheads. Tentatively, he calls out, "Is there anybody there? Can I help you? Do you require assistance?" But the water goes on rippling. The silence continues. He waits, just in case someone surfaces. They don't. Is this 'an incident' he wonders. He has been told to make sure he notes down all incidents on the report he will have to submit later. So, he leans against a convenient wall, fishes out his notebook, licks his pencil and writes down what has, or has not, happened. Then he closes the notebook and makes his way back to his beat.

The young constable is puzzled. He is not a fool. He knows he heard something unusual. He has been patrolling this beat for a couple of weeks. He has never heard anything being dropped into the dock. He has just reached the bottom of Union Street when he feels a light touch on his sleeve.

"Ello Mr P'liceman," says a soft female voice, oozing seduction. "You looking for a bit of fun?"

Cook glances down. A pair of green eyes are regarding him coquettishly from under a battered bonnet adorned with bright pink and green plumage that surely has never grown on any avian species. Cook recognises the type ~ she is one of the women his mother warned him about. Since starting out as a beat constable, he has met many 'soiled doves' as they are called. He has had numerous 'offers'. None of which ever feature in his weekly letter home.

"No. And I am on duty," he says sternly, removing his arm from her glove. (Under the aforementioned ***General Regulations, Instructions, and Orders***, he is also charged with preventing the solicitation of prostitutes.)

The bonetted one grins. "Can't blame a girl for trying," she says. "Well, Mr On Duty P'liceman, wanna hear a funny story then?"

Cook sighs. "If it's the one about the chorus girl and the Tory MP, I've heard it," he says, assuming an air of world-weariness.

She shakes her head. "Nah, this is a true story: There was two men, all muffled up. They was pushing barrows. In the barrows was a load of sacks and stuff. They took the sacks down to the river. And then they came back, and the barrows was empty. Now, ain't that funny?"

Cook stares at her. "When did this happen?" he asks.

"Just a while back. I saw them. Followed for a bit. Just outta curiosity. What you make of it?"

He shakes his head. "I don't know."

"Neevah do I. But there you are. Oh well, better be on my way. 'Night Mr On Duty P'liceman. Any time you're off duty, call in at the Dog & Diamond and ask for Temp'rance ~ that's me. Always happy to help a nice young man ... if you know what I mean." Temperance gives him a saucy wink before sauntering off, swinging her hips seductively, leaving the young constable to get out his notebook and start scribbling in it again as fast as he can.

Meanwhile, also under cover of darkness, six reliable constables, wearing heavy gloves, carrying dark lanterns and wooden hurdles have made their way to the spot where the three dead bodies were observed. They are accompanied by Greig, the surgeon Felix Lawrence (who has been dragged from his bed and ordered to attend because Greig is damned if he is going to take full responsibility for the spread of this disease), and the hapless Professor Summerton, whose hopes of returning to his book-lined room have been temporarily stymied.

Luckily for all concerned, the bodies of the three derelicts seem to have remained largely undiscovered ~ although signs of animal attack are evident. Under Greig's instructions, the corpses are carefully rolled in stout cloths, slid onto the hurdles, and taken away. They will be buried in haste in one of the parochial cemeteries. The constables will be paid extra wages and sworn to secrecy. The Professor (and his canine companions) will be allowed to catch the morning train to Oxford, having been similarly warned not to speak of what has happened. And Greig fervently hopes that this will finally be the end of the matter.

****

As dawn streaks the sky, and while Summerton is being driven to the station to catch the first train out of London, the three-man crew of the Sally-B arrive at the boat's moorings, walk along the jetty, go aboard the vessel, and prepare to set sail. The Sally-B is a small pleasure craft that plies its trade up and down the Thames, loading goods from one boat and transferring them to another, taking paying passengers for a trip along the river, and occasionally moving individuals who desire to leave the country for various reasons downriver to Gravesend to meet one of the big cross-channel steamers.

The mooring rope is untied from one of the bollards on the quay, thrown and coiled on the deck. Then two of the men start to haul up the anchor. There follows a brief hiatus as it appears to have caught on something heavy. The crew haul away until finally the anchor breaks the surface. Peering over the railings, they see that the prongs of the anchor have become entangled with a waterlogged sack. As they haul a bit more, it breaks the surface, bringing the sack with it. It lolls over each side, like panniers on the side of a donkey. The men grab a couple of poles, lean over and attempt to throw it off. Suddenly, the sack splits in two, revealing its contents. Horror stricken, the crew of the Sally-B stare over the side of the boat as what are, very clearly, human bones and skulls fall out, splashing into the murky water of the dock below.

****

The day arrives, the sun looking down like a dead face out of the sky. Nevertheless Jasper Broxton, entrepreneur and future inheritor of the Broxton estates and fortune, has awoken in a jovial mood. Yesterday, he secured an unexpected interest in his new venture. It seems that drains and sewers are very much the new investment portal. Everyone wants to buy into them. It's like the railway boom all over again.

He sends up a silent prayer of gratitude to Mr Bazalgette and the Metropolitan Board of Works who between them have pulled his irons out of the fire. Broxton now has the wherewithal to pay off the most pressing of his creditors. He has had a most satisfying meeting with his bank manager, who was almost obsequious in his demeanour ~ no folded arms and steely gaze and reminder that the bank could foreclose on his business if they chose to.

After quitting the bank, he enjoyed a fine dinner at his club, followed by an evening's entertainment at an exclusive little establishment in Mayfair, where the lady inhabitants are always sensitive to his needs and requirements. Unlike his wife, who has (both metaphorically and in reality) padlocked herself and the door to her boudoir. He didn't get back until the early hours, when the house was dark and silent, which increasingly is the time he likes it best.

Thus, Broxton rises from his single bed with a song in his heart. His clothes have been laid out for him. Fresh linen awaits. A knock at the door heralds the maid with his shaving water. He can smell bacon wafting up from below. The day stretches before him, with all its opportunities to expand and exploit. Arriving in the breakfast room, Broxton greets Avice his wife, and Johanna his daughter, who are breaking their fast in their usual manner: his wife is posting small squares of buttered toast into her mouth; his daughter is cramming bacon and eggs into hers.

Jasper Broxton helps himself from the sideboard. The parlour maid pours his coffee. He drops three sugar lumps into the cup and stirs it vigorously, his wife regarding him sourly from the far end of the oval rosewood table.

"Now then, you two," he says jovially, "what have you got planned for today?"

Johanna frowns. She has no 'plans' other than surviving mathematics, geography, scripture, and english ~ which today will involve reciting in class a truly dreadful poem called *The Lays of Ancient Rome*, which they have been learning by heart. It has LXX verses, which is LXIX verses too many for her liking. She bends over her plate, filling her mouth in the hope that she won't have to respond, even though she knows that good table manners feature high on her mother's list of 'things that are important for a young lady to display' and speaking with food in one's mouth is at the top of the list. It is unlikely, Johanna gathers, that any young man will want to court her if she devolves from the list. As if she cares.

Ignoring her, Jasper Broxton wets a finger, lifts the toast crumbs from his plate to his mouth and turns to his wife. "I have decided that you may order a new dress after all," he says. "I did a good bit of business yesterday, and I have transferred some money into the account." He waits for the expression of gratitude. While he is waiting, and Avice is gripping her jaws so tightly that she can feel stabbing pains running up the sides of her face, the parlour maid enters, bearing a silver tray.

"Letter for you, madam," she says, lowering the tray so that Avice can pick up the missive. She works a thumb under the edge, opens it and scans the contents. Next minute, her husband and daughter are treated to the terrifying sight of Avice screaming and laughing at the same time. She rises and throws the letter in the direction of her beloved. It lands in the butter. "New dress? Hahahaha. You fool! You utter fool! So much for all your boasting!"

Jasper Broxton leans across the table and whisks the letter out of the butter dish.

"See? See?" Avice cries, points a shaking index finger at him. "There is a daughter after all! We are going to inherit nothing! NOTHING!" and holding her handkerchief to her face, she rushes from the room, leaving her husband and daughter staring after her in complete bewilderment.

****

To understand Avice Broxton's dramatic behaviour, we must pause for a moment, and revert to Miss Lucy Landseer, and her search for the missing Broxton heiress. Realising that Revd. Ichabod E. Sproule is probably not going to supply her with the new address of the Asylum for Female Orphans, due to a clear prejudice against both her profession and sex, she cunningly enlists the help of her Cambridge professor. A brisk communication requesting the information, signed in his name with his relevant academic qualifications attached, results in, almost by return of post, an obsequious missive containing the relevant address.

Lucy decides to seize time by the forelock (a favourite expression of her father), and after checking in her Bradshaw, she catches a train, and in no time finds herself standing outside the forbidding wrought iron gate set in the high wall that encloses the grounds of a large house with stone dressings and coloured brickwork, located a short walk from Streatham Hill Station.

A sign informs the passer-by or prospective visitor that this is the Martha Carey Asylum for Female Orphans ~ Martha Carey, Lucy has discovered, being the philanthropist who has funded the new building. The sign also indicates that the Matron in charge is a Mrs. C. Kitterbell, and that all inquiries should be directed to her.

Lucy pulls on the bell rope attached to the wall. After a sufficient wait, she sees the front door open and a small fluffy-haired child in a light blue frock and white pinafore descend the steps and walk solemnly along the gravel drive towards the gate. She inquiries of Lucy what she wants, and having been told that Lucy has an appointment with the Matron, the cherub takes a key out of her pocket and unlocks the gate.

The small orphan leads the way to a spacious hall, with a floor of varnished pine. The walls are unpainted and devoid of any artworks. Lucy is invited to wait. She waits. Word spreads rapidly that there is a visitor, and a succession of girls, clad in the same blue dresses and pinafores appear, regard her curiously and disappear again. Lucy hears the sound of music. Upon inquiry, she is told it is one of the older girls practicing the harmonium, 'for to play in Chapel on Sunday'.

Lucy goes on waiting patiently. More orphan girls find reasons to cross the hall and take a look at her. She rewards their curiosity with a polite smile, feeling rather like one of the animals in the Zoological Gardens. She hears the words 'no sweets' uttered in a disappointed tone. Eventually a short, bustling woman in a dark dress appears, her hair neatly pinned around her head. She walks in a firm-of-purpose way and the girls skitter and vanish at her approach. The woman holds Lucy's letter in one hand.

"Miss Landseer? Good day to you. I am Mrs Kitterbell, the Matron here. Welcome to the Martha Carey Asylum for Female Orphans. I trust you had a pleasant journey? Good. I must apologise for keeping you waiting. Some matters needed my oversight. Now, if you would care to follow me, we will go straight to my sitting room."

Lucy follows the Matron through a dining-hall furnished with long tables, and smelling of every institutional dinner she has ever eaten. White-enamelled bowls and platters are piled on a dresser, awaiting use. The Matron's sitting room is a small room with French windows leading out to a lawned space with a swing or two and a trapeze hanging from a tree. The room itself is simply furnished, painted a light cream, with a desk, a crimson carpet on the varnished boards and the portrait of a woman in a skirt, a tailored jacket and a high cravat and striped tie. She is wearing a pince-nez. Lucy presumes this is the ubiquitous Martha Carey. She looks truly formidable.

The Matron sits behind her desk, Lucy sits in front of it. Vague wisps of memory curl into her mind: offences committed; admissions exacted; punishments administered. The disappointed face of her father. The Matron opens a folder, then looks up and unexpectedly smiles.

"The care of orphan girls is different from that of boys, you understand, Miss Landseer. Our primary duty has always to be to protect them from the evils that surround them, while preparing them for the part that women must take in forming the national character. Our benefactress has recently added a beautiful chapel to the grounds, a fitting crown to our work with these poor unfortunate girls. Thanks to her generosity, we are now able to instruct our charges in the duties of the Christian life."

Lucy nods. She has the feeling that this is a set speech, and until it is finished, she won't be able to explain her presence.

"Our benevolent new founder has provided them with fresh air, nourishing food, clean water and a good education," the Matron goes on. "She has spared no expense to make this a comfortable home for the poor abandoned ones. I am happy to let you peruse the recent report from the Government Inspector who declared that our girls are proficient in reading, writing and basic mathematics. We find domestic places in respectable homes for all of them when they reach maturity, and of course they are always welcome back when they are between situations."

Lucy agrees that it is indeed an impressive institution and clearly the inhabitants are lucky to live here. She hopes the Matron is on the final page.

"We are aware that our girls originally come from ~ let us say, a superior station in life. Even though fate has decreed that they have had to accommodate themselves to a different sphere," the Matron continues. "Now, Miss Landseer, you did not mention, in your letter, the reason for your visit. Am I to assume that you are seeking a girl to take into your household as parlour maid, or maybe a personal ladies' maid? I can recommend several of our girls who will only require a little more training from yourself to suit."

Lucy assumes a solemn facial expression. She lowers her eyes and her voice and launches into her own prepared statement. She describes the tragic parting between the young, seduced, betrayed mother and her new-born baby ~ her writerly talent giving her words the necessary pathos ~ and explains that the unfortunate mother, (who has NEVER married, being far too stricken with grief to commit herself elsewhere) is now unwell, and wishes to be reconciled with her only child before going to meet her Maker. She has spent time crafting this response, on the basis that admitting up front that the reconciliation is largely required to ensure an inheritance does not pass to someone else in the family, is unlikely to elicit the information her client wants.

The Matron hears her out in silence. Then, "I thank you for your candour, Miss Landseer. We try not to burden our charges with the sins of their parents. They will have enough adversity to cope with as they grow. It is not unknown for a mother whose circumstances have altered to reclaim the child she abandoned. You say you have the exact date that the child was left outside our former orphanage. That may well help us to work out which girl it could have been. Or at least narrow it down."

"And there is a shawl and a locket as well."

"That too. Although some considerable time has elapsed, time that has included a substantial change of premises, so I do not hold out much hope of the tokens being still in our possession. But of course, all things are possible. Now, I shall tell cook to provide you with some tea, which you are welcome to drink here, while I go and see if I can lay my hands upon the relevant registration ledgers for the year you mention. I believe they are stored somewhere, but I shall have to ask the bursar, who probably knows where to find them. You must understand, this is an unusual request, so please bear with us." The Matron rises. "You are free to stroll in the grounds, Miss Landseer. It is a fine afternoon, and we encourage the girls to make the most of the fresh air. If you will excuse me, I shall leave you for a time. Hopefully, I'll return shortly with good news for you."

The door closes upon her. Lucy remains seated for a while, then curiosity gets the better of her and she moves quietly to stand behind the Matron's desk. Resisting the urge to explore the drawers ~ they are nothing to do with her business here after all, she looks out into the grounds, where a group of girls are playing catch with a red rubber ball. They seem happy enough, she thinks, recalling her own childhood, much of it spent in her bedroom in disgrace over some fault or another.

Once again, her mind drifts back to Jane Eyre ~ the myth of the happy family is something she has become all too well acquainted with since she began work as a private detective. So many secrets, so much silent suffering lurks behind closed front doors. Lucy has heard it all: tales of infidelity, of cruelty, of abandonment, of promises made and broken. That is probably why she has chosen to make sure she can always support herself, never to be beholden to any man. It has inevitably meant a rift with her own family. But she does not regret it.

She returns to her seat and gets out her notebook. While she is waiting, she might as well write up the visit. She has already sent a letter to Miss Broxton suggesting a meeting at her office, to review how matters are proceeding, which is slowly, but she is not going to share that. She is deep in her efforts when the door opens, and the Matron re-appears carrying a large ledger.

"Now, Miss Landseer, you are in luck. The Bursar has rummaged through the archives and found this. I believe it covers the month you mentioned. I regret that it seems to have suffered slightly from the flood we had at the old premises, but most of the entries are still legible." She places the ledger on her desk. "I invite you to explore it."

Lucy rises and begins to turn the musty pages. The water damage is considerably more that the Matron suggested ~ many pages are stained and crumble as she turns them. Eventually she reaches the month she is seeking. Then the week. The Broxton baby was left on a Wednesday ~ her client is absolutely sure of it. There are seven entries for the first two weeks. Lucy eliminates four of them immediately as too old: the word 'infant' is used. The other three use the term 'baby'. There is no mention of any locket, although three of the girls have the word token listed against their name. Dorcas, Anne, and Ruth were passed from their birth mothers to the orphanage with only the briefest of mentions to mark their passage. Her face falls. She does not know what she hoped to find, but this is not it.

"I see you are disappointed Miss Landseer," the Matron observes. "Perhaps if the lady you represent were able to visit and actually meet the girls, she might recognise in the features of one of them something of a family resemblance to her own? I think I would be willing to permit that to happen, provided the girls were not made aware of the reason for the visit. We do not like to raise false hopes, as I'm sure you understand."

I should have thought of that, Lucy reflects, as she thanks the Matron and prepares to leave, the names of the girls listed in her notebook for future reference. She has pursued this inquiry as far as she can go. Now it is time for Miss Broxton and her sister to step into the ring. On her return to 122A Baker Street, Lucy composes a letter to her client, outlining what she has discovered, and recommending that she, and if she is well enough, her sister should pay a visit to the Orphanage, on the conditions set out by the Matron. She lists the names of the three girls who might be the abandoned child, and subtly infers that she cannot see how to proceed at this point without further information.

It is the contents of this missive that has now been sent to Avice Broxton. The letter has come, of course, from her servant spy, secreted in the enemies' house. Her regular updates have been keeping Avice abreast of the failing health of Margaret Broxton and feeding her hopes of the goodies to come. The letter does not specifically identify the future Broxton heiress; it merely repeats what was clearly a conversation between the two sisters, in which the elder Miss Broxton enlightened the younger as to the results so far of the search she has initiated.

But the mere mention of the child is enough to shatter all Avice's mounting hopes and dreams. For so many years she has secretly nurtured the vision of herself as the owner of Broxton Hall, riding out in her new shiny brougham to greet her tenants. She has plotted a wonderful future for her son Shedleigh, in which their newly inherited wealth secures him a safe seat in Parliament and a bride from a well-established noble family ~ although she might at a pinch consider one of the new American heiresses who have lately started to appear in the society columns of the newspapers.

As for her daughter Johanna, her plainness and gaucheries would be smoothed away by an expensive French finishing school, from which she would return at eighteen, ready to be launched onto the marriage market like some sleek graceful swan. It has all been planned, so much so that Avice actually believes it will happen. Or rather she did, until the unfortunate letter plopped onto the mat.

Left to contemplate her mother's empty chair, now dramatically lying on its side, Johanna Broxton looks to her father for enlightenment. None is forthcoming. Instead, she is told roughly to finish her breakfast and go to school. Johanna is aware of the inheritance of course, she could hardly fail to be, given her parents' constant harping on about it and all the things her mother says she is going to have once it arrives. Now it looks as if there is to be no inheritance to inherit after all. No nice dresses, no treats, no lording it over her contemporaries. She stuffs the last of her toast into her mouth, then grabs her hat and coat from the maid and quits the house in a rage. As the carriage carries her through the morning traffic, she works on her grievances, so that by the time she is dropped at the school gate, she is seething with resentment against her parents, her aunts, and the world in general.

After taking out her resentment by a vicious physical attack upon the two youngest members of the school, Johanna slouches into her classroom, and drops her schoolbag onto the floor next to her desk. The scowl on her face could stop a coach and four. Barely paying attention to the teacher, she runs over in her mind all the things she was promised ~ PROMISED by her mother. It is SO unfair! She is brought back to the present by the class teacher mentioning her name.

"And the name of the student from this class selected to represent her fellow pupils in the Poetry Competition is Johanna Broxton. Well done, Johanna. I am sure you won't let your classmates down."

Johanna blinks. What fresh hell is this? She turns to her desk companion, "Competition?"

"You remember: the Lays of Ancient Rome ~ the boring poem we've been learning. There's going to be a school recital this afternoon. The teachers are choosing one girl from each class to do it. And it looks like it's you. Good luck. You're going to need it," she grins wickedly. Johanna Broxton's idleness is well-known amongst her contemporaries.

Johanna slumps back into her seat. Somehow, between now and this afternoon, she is going to have to cultivate a bad headache. Either that or face total humiliation in front of the whole school.

****

Meanwhile, Ackroyd and Guskett, flushed with the success of their midnight operation, have rolled up early to open the building site to the tourist crowd. Realising that little or no profitable work is going to be done for a few days, Anton Guskett has eschewed recruiting in the poverty purlieus of the city, where those desperate to earn a pittance lurk. His man in Liverpool has written that he has collected a gang of Irish navigators, whom he intends to walk down to the capital (the cheapest route).

Ever mindful of the balance of their accounts, and the loss of a few days' income, Anton Guskett has placed advertisements in select newspapers inviting Londoners to seize this once-in-a-lifetime opportunity to view the ancient medieval walls of the city, where, it is suggested, Roman centurions once stood on guard against barbarian hordes from the north, and Medieval Kings and Queens strolled past, their spectral presence still hovering over the area. It is a masterpiece of fictive inaccuracy.

In anticipation of Londoners' love of spectacle, he has also set up a small booth just inside the site entrance, where, for a reasonable sum, visitors can purchase a ticket. As the queues build and the cashbox fills, Guskett's smirk takes on Cheshire cat proportions. A potentially disastrous situation has been pulled back from the brink, thanks to his swift and ingenious intervention.

Ackroyd, wearing a tweed jacket, workman's overalls, and a cloth cap for authenticity, but both far too clean to actually be authentic, directs the tourists to the relevant parts of the site and keeps an eye out for souvenir hunters. By dusk, when the last of the visitors has left, the two men betake themselves to a nearby hostelry to toast their successful day.

Placing the cashbox on the table, Guskett orders up two plates of roast beef and the best brandy the inn can supply. "Now then, Edward," he grins. "What did I tell you?"

Truthfully, Ackroyd isn't sure. Guskett has told him so many things. They wind themselves round inside his brain like tangled string. He takes a long drink, feeling the warming liquid easing his dry throat. Undeterred by his silence, Guskett continues,

"In a few days, our new navvies will arrive from Liverpool. I have arranged lodgings for them well away from the area, so they won't come into contact with any of the former men. I've drawn up our bid for the next contract ~ and the money from our new investor will arrive in our bank in the next few days. We have weathered the storm and now sail in sunny waters, my friend. Calm sea and prosperous voyage. See ~ as I told you, you were worried about nothing. As usual. Just leave everything to me."

****

There is a Scottish saying about the 'best laid plans of mice and men ganging aft aglay'. And so it falls out that as Jack Cully is working his way through the reports of the night constables, and trying not to wince at the desperately bad spelling and punctuation, a message arrives at the front desk that the presence of a senior detective is requested down at the Docks. Urgently. It is signed by one of the officers from the local police house.

Seizing the opportunity to be away from his desk for a while, Cully makes his way over to the Dock area, where on the jetty, he finds Sergeant William Moore, a couple of his men and three ashen-faced sailors. At their feet are two sodden fraying sacks, the contents of which have spilled. Moore steps forward and greets his colleague, his expression grim.

"'Morning, detective. Decided to send for one of you lot as this is a bit out of our range. Pilfering, illegal landing of goods, bar brawls, domestic quarrels, the odd knifing ~ we can do. Sackfulls of human bones, we can't. And anyway, even if we could, I'm short-handed at the moment, so maybe you can take this over? Crew say they hauled one sack up with the anchor this morning. Wasn't there yesterday when they tied up. They fished this lot out after. They think there are more sacks down there too ~ they had a poke around with a pole. So, I decided to bring in the big boys from Scotland Yard."

Somewhere in Cully's brain, a small light starts flashing on and off. Sacks. He is sure he read something about sacks very recently ... but where? He turns to the three crew members of the Sally-B who are now standing so close together they look as if they are trying to form one composite person.

"Gentlemen ...?" he says interrogatively, always a winning opening as it leaves the field wide open for any interpretation. He waits, notebook at the ready. There is some foot-shuffling. Then two of the crew take a step back, leaving the third, the captain, Cully presumes, unprotected. A fish out of water, as it were.

"Yes ...?" Cully says gently.

"It's like this," the hapless man flounders, "we were on our way downriver: got a steamer to meet, when it happened. Honest to God, officer, it's nothing to do with us. We nivver saw them sacks before. We nivver dumped them in the river. We didn't see anyone. We didn't hear anyfink. We're just hard-working mariners."

"I believe you," Cully says, and the relief in the man's eyes is almost palpable.

"Can we be on our way then?"

Cully nods, at which the sailor turns to his two companions, and they all scuttle off down the jetty, almost throwing themselves onto the deck of the Sally-B. He watches them cast off, then swing the boat out of the dock and disappear downriver at speed.

"So, detective," Moore says, folding his arms, "what now? Where do we go from here? Or rather, where do you go? I have a hundred and one things I should be attending to."

Cully is staring at the piles of long bones, ribcages, and skulls. "They don't look very recent, do they?" he murmurs, frowning. "From the state of them, I'd say they've been wherever they've been for quite a long time. Before they were dropped in the river, that is."

"Take your word for it. I don't pretend to be an expert on old bones. Question is, what are you going to do with them ~ because they can't stay here, that's for sure. I know my patch and it won't be long before it gets out that there's a load of human remains on the quayside and then I'll have half the neighbourhood down here gawping. And I really don't want that."

Cully agrees. He doesn't want that either. "If you could please arrange for the bones to be taken to Scotland Yard, I'd like to get our police surgeon to take a look at them. He might be able to say how recently they were interred."

Moore sighs. Rolls his eyes. Then he beckons to his constables. "Right lads. You heard the detective. Nip along to the coal merchants. Tell them Sergeant Moore wants some sacks. Clean sacks. Big sacks. Probably at least two. Say it's police business and I'll settle up later. Nothing more. Understood? Bring the sacks here. Fill them with the bones and skulls. Take the sacks to Scotland Yard. Chop, chop ~ we haven't got all day!"

Cully walks off. He needs to warn Robertson what is about to land on his dissecting table. But as he walks back to Scotland Yard, the question still remains. Circling round in his brain. Sacks? He knows there is something about sacks that is important but alas, it is currently eluding him.

****

Having quit the *dulce domum* in a rage at the unwelcome news that a putative heiress to the Broxton fortune has been discovered, Jasper Broxton arrived at his office, snarled at his clerk, before penning a quick missive to his lawyer, and as a result, here he is now, sitting on an uncomfortable cliental chair in the cold office of Lillerton Grind of Grind, Grippe and Holde. The office is situated in Lincoln's Inn, up a flight of steep stone stairs. The window on the first-floor landing looks out over an abandoned graveyard. In the front office, a lawyer's clerk scratches away with a quill, and coughs at intervals.

Lawyer Lillerton Grind sits behind a big wooden desk, on a high-backed black chair with rows of brass-studded nails, like a coffin. He steeples his long talon fingers as he regards his client with hard steely grey eyes. His swooping nose resembles the beak of some predatory bird. He reads Broxton's letter, then reaches for the Broxton folder, opens it and begins reading.

"Hmm ... hmm ... yes. Yes ... hmm," he murmurs thoughtfully, turning the pages.

Jasper Broxton stirs uneasily in his seat. He is hoping for a swift solution to the current crisis. A way of returning to the status quo, coupled with some legal pit down which he can throw his two cousins. He waits. A fly buzzes aimlessly against the glass. The clerk coughs. A distant church bell chimes. Grind reads on. Eventually he lifts his head. Nods to himself a couple of times.

"Interesting. Yes. An *interesting* development."

"But not a hope in hell, eh? It's not a possibility, is it? They are trying to deceive us. There cannot be an actual child, can there? It is a fake."

A pause.

"Well now, let us consider the facts. The Broxton inheritance is passed down through the female line from mother to daughter. An unusual method, but not an unknown one. As it currently stands, the younger of the two sisters was designated by her maternal parent to be the next inheritor of the title and all that pertains to it. If ~ and I emphasise the use of the conditional, if, as I say, there was a female child born to Margaret Broxton, and its provenance can be established, then she is within her right, under law, to declare said child the future benefactory of her properties and monies."

Jasper Broxton's face turns red. His hands curl into fists. "But, Hell and Damnation! The woman was never married! The child is a bastard!"

"Nevertheless," Lawyer Grind continues smoothly, "although that would undoubtedly be the case, and however unfortunate her situation in the face of society's moral expectations, the Broxton inheritance passes from mother to daughter. I have read through every document and Will carefully and there is no mention of the marital status of the maternal parent. None whatsoever. Therefore, whether your cousin married or remained single is not germane to the issue. On the balance of probability, and taking into account previous case law, a court would find in favour of the child."

Jasper Broxton utters a howl of fury. The lawyer's expression remains neutral. The disappointment of clients is an everyday event, and he has acquired, over the years, the ability to detach himself completely from their sufferings.

"So, what do you suggest I should do now?" Broxton hisses between gritted teeth.

The lawyer strokes the side of his beak with a foreclaw while he considers the question ~ in that he considers the most tactful way of saying you've had it, chum. There are his fees to consider, and he has already had to request payment twice for the last consultation.

"The existence of the female child is the stumbling block here. The absence of the aforementioned girl would mean that the Broxton inheritance would devolve, by default, to your family, as the law pertaining to this matter dictates." He closes his mouth firmly. Gathers the documents together in a 'that's it' manner.

Jasper Broxton sits in silent contemplation for a couple of seconds. Then he rises, claps his top hat on his head, utters a brief word of thanks and bidding Grind good day, barrels through the front office and out into the street, the lawyer's words ringing in his ears: *the absence of the girl*. He hails a cab and orders the driver to take him to his office. *The absence of the girl* … it couldn't be clearer: if there is no girl, then he inherits everything. Therefore somehow, and he isn't yet sure how he will accomplish it, he is going to make damn sure that there will be no girl.

****

While her beloved husband is receiving legal enlightenment from his lawyer, Avice Broxton is seeking enlightenment from her own source. Here she is once again, lurking in the doorway opposite the town house where Margaret Broxton and her sister reside. The fury she is currently directing towards the house is so great that it is a wonder that any of the windows remain intact. Avice usually doesn't see anybody during her daily vigils. So, she is surprised when a closed carriage draws up, and after a short wait, the two sisters emerge, cloaked and bonetted, the older supporting the younger. They climb into the carriage and are driven off.

She waits awhile just in case they return. When they fail to reappear, Avice crosses the road and pulls on the bell rope. She is in luck: the door is opened by her servant spy. Laying a finger to her lips, Avice indicates that she will remain in the street for the servant to join her. She turns and walks on a few yards. When she hears the sound of footsteps behind her, she continues walking until she reaches the corner of the street, where she halts. The servant joins her.

"Nobody saw you leave the house, did they?" Avice asks.

"I told Cook I had an 'eadache and was just popping out for a bit of fresh air."

Avice nods. "Good. Good. I see they have gone out."

"They've gone to the orphanage to meet the girls what I wrote you of."

Avice tries not to wince. Had this been Johanna her daughter and not some lowly servant, she'd have issued a lecture on the use and importance of correct grammar. However.

"I will need you to discover whatever you can about this meeting. It is very important," she says, trying not to notice the sudden wild plunge in her stomach.

"I will." The servant nods. She is giving a very good impression of somebody trying her hardest to oblige. There is a pause. "Anything else?"

Avice opens her bag and shakes out some coins into her gloved hand. Loyalty, (or disloyalty depending upon which side of the green baize door you are on) has its price. She gives the coins over with a faked smile. The servant nods her thanks and pockets the money. Then she spins on her heel and walks off smartly. As Avice watches her go, her features seem to swirl and reshape themselves into a different, crueller face.

****

It is afternoon when Jack Cully receives the message that his presence is requested by Robertson, the Scotland Yard police surgeon, indicating that Moore has been as good as his word and sent the sacks of bones. Cully makes his way over to the cold, white-washed mortuary which is located across a courtyard from the main building. It is a windowless room, with wooden shelving laden with bottles and glass-stoppered jars containing things that he'd rather not think about.

At the centre of the room, is the scrubbed metal table with its various drainage outlets and, laid out on a bench nearby, the tools of the surgeon's trade: saws, drills, and various serrated knives. Robertson and his assistant, a young fresh-faced medical student, are awaiting his arrival. As usual, the police surgeon's saturnine face wears its sarcastic expression.

"Ah, detective ~ we have received your delivery, with thanks. Quite brightened up what was, until then, a rather boring morning. We were thinking we might have to resort to re-labelling our collections of specimens, were we not, Anstruther? Have you met young Anstruther, detective inspector? The latest of my young acolytes. Fresh from medical school and eager to master the craft of post-mortem dissection."

The young man in the white coat smiles uneasily. It is clear that he hasn't yet mastered how to deal with Robertson.

"So, detective, to our muttons, as our friends across the channel put it. I have examined some of the long bones and skulls you sent me, and my conclusion is that they are old. Very old indeed. From the discolouration, the size, the general wear and tear and the condition of them, I'd say we are looking at the bones of individuals who lived and subsequently died perhaps two centuries ago."

"Ah. I understand." Inwardly, Cully breathes a sigh of relief. So, they were not looking at some mass murderer roaming the city and disposing of his victims at will.

"I do not see anything to suggest violence was part of their demise, therefore I conclude that either penury, natural causes or disease was the vehicle that carried them off. The fact that all these bodies were found in the same place eliminates penury and natural causes, and makes me wonder whether what we have here, detective inspector, are the contents of one of the old city plague pits."

Cully feels a visceral fear run through him. The word plague, even at this great distance, carries the taint of families nailed up inside their houses, with red crosses and the words 'God have mercy on us' on the doors, and plague carts making their way by night through the deserted city.

"It couldn't come back, could it?" he asks. "Not after all this time."

Head on one side, Robertson considers the question. "There have been no big outbreaks of plague in the city since that time," he says. "So, I think it is possible to assume that the discovery of these bones ~ if, indeed their origins are such as I have suggested, ought not to herald another major outbreak."

Cully thanks him and turns to go.

"However," Robertson adds, ruminatively, "one must always consider the possibility that the event might be replicated."

"What?" Cully halts in the doorway.

"I merely offer an opinion, detective," the surgeon shrugs. "The runes are for you to read. God forbid ~ if you believe in a deity, of course ~ that we should endure the arrival of that particular disease in the city once again. Loth as I am to offer any advice, it is not within my bailiwick, as you know, but were I to proffer such, I might suggest you ascertain from whence these bones originated. And who has handled them in the process of removing them from their final resting place. And the health of said removers. That should provide you with the answers that I am unable to supply. Now, if that is all, given that no crime is here to be investigated, we shall arrange for the decent and timely disposal of these remains. I bid you good day."

It is a very thoughtful Jack Cully who makes his way back to his small office, where after some time spent in contemplation of the wall opposite his desk, his reverie is interrupted by a knock at the door, which opens to reveal a cautious Constable Timothy Cook.

"Yes?" Cully says, not having a clue who the young man might be.

Cook eases himself into the office. He stands in front of Cully's desk, shifting awkwardly from one foot to the other. He runs his index finger under his collar.

"Do sit down, constable," Cully says.

"If it's all right with you, I'd rather stand, sir. Helps me get my thoughts in order."

Cully's eyebrows shoot up. "I see. And what thoughts would they be? And who are you, by the way ~ I don't recall seeing you before?"

"I'm Cook, sir. Timothy Cook. Constable. Recently joined the force, sir. Moved from Whitechapel police office. Well, it's like this: I was in the front office a few hours ago, checking the rosters, sir, when I spotted a couple of men I recognised from police college coming in with some sacks, sir."

Cully suddenly focuses his gaze on the young man. "Did you indeed, constable."

"I did sir. And so I went over, friendly like, to see if they needed any assistance, and they told me they was to take the sacks straight to old Robbo ~ Mr Robertson, sorry sir, slipped out. So I asked them what was in the sacks, and they told me a heap of old bones that got fished out of the docks last night. So I thought I better come and find you, sir. You did read the report I left on your desk? Because I wrote about a member of the public who told me she'd seen two men wheeling some sacks in a couple of barrows in the direction of the docks. I thought it was a bit of a coincidence, sir. The men, and the sacks."

Of course! The sacks. Now he remembers. Cully fishes around in the pile of papers on his desk until he finds Cook's report. He skim-reads it, refamiliarizing himself with the contents. Then he stands up.

"Very good work, Constable Cook. Shame we don't know how to get in touch with the young lady. Her evidence might be vital."

A blush suffuses the young man's cheeks. "She did tell me where she was staying, sir," he says.

"Then I suggest you go and talk to her. Find out all you can. Does she know where the men came from?"

Cook bites his lower lip. "I could do that, sir, and I want to do it, believe me, but I fear she might get the wrong idea ~ if you see what I mean, sir."

Cully suppresses a smile. The days when he was propositioned by young women in the street are long gone, but not so long gone that he can't remember them. "Would it help if I accompanied you?" he suggests. "I have some specific things I'd like to ask the young lady myself."

"It would, sir. Thank you, sir," Cook pauses, "but why is it important, sir? A heap of old bones ~ they can't be part of some crime, can they?"

Cully takes a breath. "They might be," he says. "And that's all I can tell you right now. So let us go. The sooner we get to the bottom of this strange business, the better."

Even seen through the glow of gaslight and a lot of alcohol, the Dog & Diamond is not a picturesque hostelry. In broad daylight its shoddy interior presents few attractions, which might be why Cully and the young officer find themselves entering an empty bar. A surly-looking man with bitten fingernails who is wiping the bar with a greyish cloth, glances up as they approach.

"Ain't got no more grub left, gents," he greets them.

Cully explains that they are not in need of sustenance but wish to talk to a young lady called Temperance, at which the landlord looks slyly from him to Cook and grins.

"Werl now, Temp'rance is it? Hur, hur, hur ~ not known her do two at a time before, hur, hur, hur. Must be branchin' out."

Cully produces his warrant card. The grin disappears rapidly. "Along to your left, froo the door and up the stairs. I know she was there a while ago coz I took her up some gin," he grunts, and resumes wiping the bar.

It takes a while for Temperance to understand that her services are required upon an extra-mural matter, then to agree to the purpose of their visit. However, once she grasps that nothing more is needed than that she walks them back along the route taken by the two mysterious men with the barrows, and that compliance with their request would be in her best interest, as failure to do so could see her up before a magistrate for soliciting an officer on duty, she wraps herself in a shawl, puts on the battered bonnet and the three of them set off, using the rear entrance of the pub.

Temperance walks ahead, followed at a decent distance by Cully and Cook. "Acoz I don't want any of me regulars seein' me with a couple of p'licemen. I got my reputation to fink of," she explains to them. When she reaches the place where she first spotted the two men, she stops, points to it, then wheels round and heads off, leaving Cully and Cook standing on the footway, looking around them for inspiration. Cully makes a quick inventory. They are in the middle of a street of houses. The source of the sacks could be in any direction and there are only the two of them here. He needs back-up, a plan, and a map.

"When do you go off duty?" he asks.

The young constable looks off. "Three hours ago, sir ~ but it doesn't matter. Only too glad to help you, sir."

Cully groans inwardly. The young man will probably be on night patrol shortly, having had no sleep and it is his fault. He should have asked him before dragging him across town. "You go and get yourself a good supper," he says, handing over some coins. "I need to talk to Mr Greig about what we've discovered and see what he thinks about it. You've been very useful, constable, and I'll make sure I put in a report saying so."

Constable Cook beams his thanks and sets off at speed. Meanwhile Jack Cully heads in the direction of his home, letting his feet carry him while his mind mulls over the day's revelations. The very idea that London could be threatened by an outbreak of plague is beyond his comprehension. He consoles himself with the thought that, as he has heard nothing, it seems unlikely. Even so, those who might have exposed thousands of people to a terrible and fatal disease need to be caught and punished. Tomorrow, he will make it his business to select some reliable men and scour the area. Every building site. Every back yard. They will not escape. Reaching the small, terraced house at last, he is greeted by Emily and his youngest daughter.

"Where's Violet?" he inquires, seeing only three places laid in the kitchen.

Emily smiles. "She is celebrating winning the Poetry Recitation with her friend May. They both came first in the competition this afternoon. May's mother is cooking a special Italian supper for them. Her father will bring Violet back later. I said you would not mind ~ she was so excited."

Cully nods. "She's made a good friend there," he says, easing off his boots. "Was that the poem about some captain who stood on a bridge? She's been saying bits of it to me for weeks. And explaining how to count in Latin. Can't say I understood it all."

Emily nods. She bends down and lifts a fragrant steak pie out of the oven. "She and May were allowed to recite a verse each, as they are the youngest. None of the other girls managed to recall the whole poem and one girl, an older one, could only remember three verses! The headmistress was not well pleased with them."

Cully goes to wash his hands at the sink. His bright girl. He is so proud of her.

****

There is a tavern in the town. And there, the students from various medical schools and hospitals go to sit them down, compare gruesome stories and drink themselves into various states of stupor. Sometimes they bring in the odd skeleton, or skull, and insist it needs a drink as well. The pub is known amongst the student fraternity as the 'Sawbones Arms', and thanks to their jolly japes and their inclination to discuss aspects of their trade loudly and in detail, it is now almost entirely frequented by medical students and newly qualified hospital doctors.

Here is a group of merry pranksters. Having joshed with the landlord (who has the patience of a saint), they have taken their pint pots to a quiet corner (in that there aren't any), and are now debating the symptoms of advanced syphilis. Loudly. Suddenly, the door is flung open. The newcomer is hailed and invited to join them.

"Anstruther! My good man!" one of the group shouts over the noise in the bar, waving his pot and swaying in his seat. "How does the world go with thee?" (Sometime in the future, this man will be a famous army surgeon, responsible for saving the lives of many soldiers on the field of combat. But this is not that day.) Anstruther, assistant to Robertson, the Scotland Yard police surgeon, strides to the bar, flirts with the barmaid, then comes back with his drink.

"Got anything interesting to show us tonight?" one of the group asks. Ever since Anstruther began his latest posting, he has been smuggling out some of the more gruesome objects kept in the morgue to simultaneously entertain his fellow students and enhance his status with them.

Anstruther has a bag with him. He opens the bag and brings out a glass bottle, which he places on the table. Inside the bottle, something curded and grey floats in a clear viscous fluid. "Section of the brain of a murderer," he says complacently. The group leans forward and studies it intently. "I wonder whether the brain of a murderer looks different to the brain of an ordinary man," the future army surgeon muses. "It would be fascinating to study them together and see."

"Happy to open up your skull, Desmond," grins another one of the group. Desmond laughs. "How do you know I do not harbour murderous thoughts?" he says. "Very interesting, Anstruther. Anything else to report?"

Anstruther looks all round furtively. The group fix their corporate gaze on him.

"Come on man, don't keep us in suspense," one of them says impatiently.

"Well," the young man says, lowering his voice in a suitably dramatic manner, "this morning we had some sacks brought in by a constable from one of the dockside police. They were full of bones …"

"Oh, bones! Don't bloody talk to me about bones! I spend my LIFE drawing bones, sorting bones, studying bones," one of the medical fraternity declares, rolling his eyes.

"Ah, maybe, but not bones like these ~ these bones came from an old plague pit ~ yes, really! Mr Robertson thinks it must've been unearthed quite recently and whoever found them, got scared and dumped them in the river."

There is an almost imperceptible leaning away from Anstruther. Perceptible in that two of the medical students move their chairs further from him and closer to the smoky interior wall of the pub.

"Look, these bones are over two hundred years old," Anstruther says. "You seriously don't think they carry any plague now? Do you?"

Wary glances are exchanged.

"Well, do you?"

"And what did the great Mr Robertson have to say upon the matter?" Desmond asks.

"He agrees the bones have been buried too long for them to be significant," Anstruther says. "I mean, think about it: two hundred years. Very unlikely, wouldn't you say?" Then honesty compels him to add, "at least he doesn't *think* there is any danger. Though he did say one must always consider the *possibility* that the event might be replicated."

There is a pause. Some awkward shifting in their seats. "Let me get everybody another drink," Anstruther says cheerfully. He rises to go to the bar, not noticing the paunchy middle-aged man in the flash waistcoat and loud tweed jacket, who is sitting at a nearby table and has been eavesdropping on the conversation for the past ten minutes.

It is said that in London you are never more than six feet away from a rat, or a journalist, which in some people's opinion, is pretty well the same thing. In this case, the 'rat' has developed the ability to lip read: an important asset in his job.

While Anstruther is buying the drinks, his friends sit in glum silence, clearly disturbed by their companion's recent revelations. Meanwhile the man in the waistcoat surreptitiously fetches a notebook from his inner jacket pocket, extracts a pencil from behind his left ear, licks the end of the pencil, and begins scribbling rapidly.

****

It is a fine sunny morning, which exactly matches the mood of ex-Detective Inspector Leo Stride as he makes his way towards Scotland Yard. Yesterday, he penned the first chapter of his book (now titled *Boots on the Ground: Memoirs of a London Detective*). Today, he intends making preliminary notes for the next chapter. He spies his favourite coffee stall, busy as usual despite the early hour, and heads towards it, a smile on his face. A mug of his favourite black treacly brew should set him up nicely for the morning ahead.

Stride greets the elderly couple manning the stall, and has just taken charge of a chipped white china mug (on a return later basis), when he is sidled up to by a rough-looking old cove in stained corduroy trousers and an out-at-the-elbows jacket that might have started out smart but has clearly lost its sartorial way since. Stride is used to being sidled up to in this way ~ it seems to be how the lower classes prefer to deal with members of his profession, so he comes to a halt and waits for the sidler to reveal his purpose.

"You that d'tctive?" the man whispers, touching his cap.

Stride affirms that, on balance, yes, he probably is.

"Fort so. Bin waiting for yer. Yeah. Ma Crocket sent me. Know who I mean?"

Stride nods, inwardly marvelling at the way the underground message service manages to function so efficiently.

"Ma says try around Whitechapel ~ vere's a building site wot is supposed to be haunted. Ain't none of the Irish will work vere no more."

"Haunted?"

"Ghosts, ghouls, dead bodies. Vat's what vey say and vat's what she told me to tell you." The sidler pauses, looking at Stride significantly. He opens a tattered pocket, and allows his gaze to stray to it, sadly. With a sigh, Stride gives him a few coins. "Please take this for your trouble, and make sure you thank Ma for me."

The sidler touches the brim of his greasy cap and wanders away. Stride takes his mug of now lukewarm coffee and enters the building. He had intended to transfer it and himself down to the basement, but first he decides he is duty-bound to pass on the information he's received to Lachlan Greig. Even if it sounds implausible. He reminds himself that it is often just such bizarre information that proves in the end to be a vital part of an investigation. And that this is not his investigation, and he is not supposed to be involved in it.

When Stride reaches Lachlan Greig's office, he finds Jack Cully already *in situ*. The two men have their heads together and are studying a map. They glance up as he enters. Stride places his mug of almost cold coffee carefully down on a corner of Greig's desk.

"I've just had a tip-off about where that ... person ... might have been working," he says cautiously. He glances at Cully, then back at Greig meaningfully, not sure how much discretion needs to be applied, not wanting to be tactless.

"It's fine. You may speak freely. Jack knows to whom we are referring. Indeed, he is now part of the investigation and has just come to see me with some important information. We have progressed since you and I last spoke," Greig says. Briefly, he outlines the basic developments: four more deaths, the sacks of bones, the possibility that they might have originated from a plague pit, and the men in the night with wheelbarrows.

Stride listens intently. Part of him yearns to be at the centre of things once more, issuing orders, watching as the various parts of the jigsaw come together to make a complete pattern. The other part of him is relieved he is not going to have to deal with any fallout, should this ever become public knowledge. Stride knows his city. When problems arise, it tends to err on the side of instant panic rather than considered reason. He waits until Greig has finished speaking, then passes on what the sidler told him. The two men exchange a significant glance.

"As it happens, we are examining a map of the Whitechapel area right now. There are several building sites that may well be pertinent to our investigation," Greig says. "We intend to search the area today. Whoever removed those bones and dumped them in the river will be brought in for questioning. We must ascertain whether there are any more bones or plague pits in the area. If there are, the whole site has to be sealed off." He nods at Stride. "Thank you for your information. It confirms what we already suspected. Now, we have a search party to organise, and we mustn't keep you from your important research."

Crushed, Stride leaves what used once to be his office. If he'd harboured any hope of being invited to join the search party, it is clear that is not going to happen. It is only when he reaches his small desk in the basement that he remembers he left his mug of coffee in Greig's office and now it is too late, and anyway, he has too much pride, to go back and get it.

****

Meanwhile, Miss Lucy Landseer arrives at her Consulting Room at 122A Baker Street to find a letter on her desk awaiting her attention. Miss Clara Broxton writes to update Miss Landseer with the progress of her search. She thanks Miss Landseer for her prompt communication. Her sister rallied slightly upon the news and together, they took a carriage ride to the Female Orphanage yesterday.

Having met with the three girls, and spoken with them for some time, it is their joint opinion that Ruth is clearly the one who was left on the Orphanage doorstep as a new-born baby so many years ago. Their decision was reached by the discovery that one of the other candidates was 'dusky-skinned', while the other, according to Miss Broxton, was 'an imbecile'.

They have now written to the Matron, and have applied formally to bring the girl to their home to get to know her better and to instruct her in those matters that pertain to her future. On behalf of Margaret and herself, she extends her gratitude to Miss Landseer for her diligent inquiries and encloses a cheque for services rendered. Yours, etc. etc.

Lucy is relieved. A new life is about to begin for one abandoned orphan. She does love a happy ending. She has written enough of them in her stories. She spends the rest of the working day catching up on paperwork, of which there is a considerable amount ~ her business is not yet so profitable that she can employ a secretary, and due to the nature of many of her investigations, she is naturally wary of entrusting very private and personal matters to another person.

At the end of the day, having banked her cheque and received no new instructions from any prospective clients, Lucy will pack her work satchel and head for home. The Case of the Missing Heiress has been an interesting case, but one way and another, she is content to see the back of it. All's well that ends well, as the playwright has it. Hopefully, she will hear nothing further from or about Miss Clara Broxton and her sister Margaret.

****

The first inkling that his greatest fear is about to be realised comes when Sir Charles Trelawney, renowned senior surgeon, and Board Member at the London Hospital, is preparing to quit the hallowed portals of his place of work with the intention of finding a cab to take him to his Club for a well-deserved luncheon. He has spent the morning in the small lecture theatre, expounding the mysteries of his craft to the latest cohort of medical students.

Over the years, Sir Charles has developed a rather dramatic style of oratory, more suited to the classical theatre than the medical fraternity, but it has proved popular with students, who hang on every flourish and florid hyperbole. Thus, his lectures are always well attended. Now, as the lecture theatre clears, he packs away his surgical saws and drills and congratulates himself on a job well done. In the afternoon, he will don his surgical attire ~ a frock coat and apron, and perform various operations, though nowadays, he only operates on selected patients, generally those whom he knows socially.

As Sir Charles crosses the atrium, he is approached by a crowd of badly dressed men with notebooks and pencils. He endeavours to skirt round them but is prevented from doing so. Instead, he finds himself hemmed in on all sides.

"What is this outrage?" he exclaims. "Where are the porters?" he continues, raising his voice to a shout. "I demand you clear the atrium of these individuals at once!!"

"Not so fast, squire," the words emanate from a man who reeks of cigar smoke and macassar oil. He proffers his card, "Richard Dandy, from *The Inquirer*, the paper that speaks for the man in the street. And what the man in the street wants to know is: what is this rumour about an outbreak of plague? Why haven't we been warned?"

The colour drains from Sir Charles' face. "I do not know what you are talking about, my good man," he stutters.

"Well, for a start, I'm not your 'good man'," Dandy responds tartly. "And I think you do know what I'm talking about, seeing as one of your own hospital porters died from it."

Sir Charles stiffens. "How on earth do you know about that?" he hisses.

"I didn't know it for sure. Just heard a rumour, which I didn't believe. But you've confirmed it now, squire. And that you knew about it and that you have done nothing. My readers are going to want answers. Their lives are in danger. Every man, woman and child in London is in danger. So, I repeat ~ why haven't you come clean?" Dandy raises his voice. Other medical staff and patients pause in their progress across the atrium, their faces betraying their horror at what is going on.

Clamping his mouth closed, Sir Charles wrenches himself free and heads for the door, the reporting pack in full pursuit. Once outside, he jumps into the nearest cab, shouting to the driver to take him to his Club. As the cab pulls away, Dandy shouts after it, "You've got blood on your hands, Sir Charles Trelawney! Blood! And you're not going to escape. We'll make quite sure of that! Oh yes!"

****

The full implications of their actions are also being made quite clear to some other individuals, for Jack Cully and his team of constables, who have been following the leads supplied by Temperance and Ma Crockett, finally show up at the construction site of Ackroyd and Guskett, where the sight of a couple of wheelbarrows containing a pile of neatly folded sacks alerts Cully that they have finally found what and whom they are looking for. As a result, both men are taken to Scotland Yard, to await interrogation.

Lachlan Greig being currently detained elsewhere, Cully orders the two men to wait on the Anxious Bench in the front office, telling the desk sergeant to keep a deliberately watchful eye on them, but to say or do nothing, on the basis that there is nothing like a bit of distanced intimidation to break down resistance.

Time passes. Ackroyd fidgets and fusses. Guskett adopts a nonchalant pose, as if being questioned by Scotland Yard's top detectives is an everyday occurrence. Eventually, they are led to an interview room, where they finally come face to face with Greig, Cully, and two inspectors from H Division (Whitechapel) who have been invited by electric telegraph to participate in the interview. It is not a particularly large room, so if they did not feel intimidated before, Ackroyd and Guskett certainly do now.

Whilst the officers spend a few moments checking they all have the same paperwork, Anton Guskett does his level best to convey the impression of a man trying his hardest to oblige. Edward Ackroyd, in contrast, just slumps in his seat, his eyes downcast, a man out of his depths and overwhelmed by events.

"Right gentlemen, shall we begin?" Greig says brisky, opening the batting for the forces of law and order. "I presume you both know why you have been brought to Scotland Yard?"

Ackroyd utters a deep and mournful sigh. He still does not raise his eyes. Guskett changes his facial expression to portray puzzled bewilderment. Greig continues: "We have reason to believe that you both, assisted by some workmen in your employ, discovered a burial site in the course of your excavations for the new sewer system, and that you dug up the remains of the bodies buried there and subsequently removed them. We have strong evidence that you secretly placed the remains in sacks and threw them into the river under cover of darkness. Anything to say?"

Ackroyd crosses and uncrosses his legs nervously.

"But when they were buried first time round, it was outside the city wall," Guskett remarks, with a smile that is taking every muscle in his body to keep on his face.

"I fail to see your point," Greig says coldly.

"My point, officer, is that tech'nically, it could be said the bodies weren't ever buried in London. So their fate isn't a matter for the London authorities today and we haven't done anything wrong."

"I doubt that would hold up in a court of law," one of the H inspectors remarks drily.

"It might," Guskett says, hopefully.

"Why did you not notify the local police force when you first came across human remains?" one of the other H inspectors asks. "Did you not consider it was your duty to do so?"

"I said so at the time," Ackroyd says, finally finding his voice, and getting a kick in the shin from his partner as a consequence.

"Look, officers," Guskett says in an 'I'm-being-perfectly-reasonable' voice, "we are on a deadline. Those new sewer pipes need to be in place as quickly as possible. The city badly needs new sewers. We all agree on that, don't we? It's a health issue. These bits and pieces of long-dead people ~ they aren't going to have friends and relations who'll care where they end up, are they? Whereas there are thousands of living people ~ families with kiddies, whose lives will be made better by not having to drink filthy water or having the contents of their cesspits running through their houses. Don't you agree?"

"Do you have any idea why the bodies you unearthed were buried outside the city walls?" Cully asks.

Both men shrug and shake their heads.

"They were plague victims," Cully says quietly, and is gratified to see a look of absolute horror cross both men's faces. "What you dug up was an old plague pit from the seventeenth century. It was the custom then for the night-carts to take dead bodies out of the city so as not to infect others."

There is a pause while the information is slowly digested.

"Now we need to ask you some questions about the men who worked on your site," Greig says. "In particular, a young man, possibly Irish. His last day working there would be ..." he consults his notes and names the day. "Do you remember this young man?"

Anton Guskett instantly shakes his head. "You see, I don't deal with the day-to-day matters on the site. That's up to my partner."

The officers focus in on Ackroyd, who sits unhappily fiddling with his watch chain.

"Sir ...?" Greig prompts.

"I might recall such a man," Ackroyd hesitates. "He was only on the site for a day. I believe ~ I'm not sure. He could possibly have been the one who was working in the area where the remains were located."

"Could have been ..."

"I believe he was, yes," Ackroyd admits unhappily. "He didn't come back the next day as far as I remember."

"No, well, he wouldn't have returned," Greig says grimly. "He was found outside the London Hospital some time later, dead. Do I need to spell out what he died from?"

Ackroyd works his mouth, bites down on his lower lip. "Surely I cannot be blamed for that?" he says, his voice now almost a whisper.

"No, you are right. You can't," Greig agrees. "But I'd now like to question you about three older men, derelicts, not young Irish navvies this time. We think they were working on the site on..." he glances down at his notes again to refresh his memory. "Do you remember these men?"

Ackroyd shoots a sharp glance at his partner. "He brought them onto the site," he says. "We needed to move the remains to finish the job, but none of the Irish would work for us as they claimed the site was haunted. So, he found these men and got them to shovel the bones into some sacks."

"Which you later disposed of by night," one of the H inspectors says. "The three men all perished from the same disease. That's four dead men."

"Five," Cully says. "The night porter at the hospital who took in the dead body of the young labourer also perished."

"Do you have ANY IDEA what your reckless actions could potentially lead to?" Greig says, raising his voice. He is standing up now, his features contorted with fury. "The population of London currently stands at just over three and a half million people. And YOU might possibly have just unleashed upon them one of the deadliest plagues ever to be seen in this country!"

Anton Guskett raises a defensive hand. "Now, hold on, hold on," he says, "we acted in good faith. We didn't know what the remains were. Yes, I'll admit, we could have reported them. And we didn't. We hold up our hands to that. But the rest? From what you've told us here in this room, there haven't been any further deaths for weeks now. And given we got rid of the remains, I don't see how anybody else could catch it. In a way, we've done you a favour ~ oh, you can glare at me if you like, but if we hadn't disposed of those bits and bones quickly, if instead, we'd reported them to the authorities like you suggested, with all the form filling and paperwork and this department and that department and such, who knows how many of your men might be dead now?" Guskett pauses to let his words sink in. "So how about letting us go ~ the sooner we finish installing the pipes on that site, the sooner everything will be covered over, and we can close it down and move on."

The silence that follows his words goes on far longer than any silence should. Then,

"You may both leave," Greig says coldly, "but know I will be writing to the Home Secretary. Until I hear from him, you are not permitted to quit London. You will leave your addresses at the front desk on your way out and you will report to my colleagues in the Whitechapel police office every day so that I know you have not tried to go anywhere. Now, get out of my sight, both of you!"

The two men rise and exit the room in single file, not making eye contact with their interlocuters. Once safely outside Scotland Yard and back on the footway, Anton Guskett turns to face his business partner. "I think that went pretty well, all things considered, don't you agree, old man?" he says, with a complacent smile. "Hopefully, that's the end of the matter as far as we are concerned. Now we can finish the job and move on to the next."

In reply, Ackroyd merely gives him a stricken look and walks quickly away.

****

Alas, despite Anton Guskett's confident assertion, the matter is far from being over. The first inkling of trouble, like whisps of smoke from a distant bonfire, arrives with the early afternoon papers. Stride is walking back to his research after a hearty luncheon when he hears the newsboys calling the headlines. In former days, he'd have had a selection of the more scurrilous papers delivered to his office so that he could stay one step ahead of whatever idiocy they were writing about and be ready to stamp on them hard before the evening editions, which will be read by millions on their way home from work, and carried, via the railway network, all over the country.

Stride pauses, conflicting options swirling in his mind. His summary dismissal from Greig's office earlier in the day makes it quite clear that he is no longer regarded as an active member of the Detective Division. On the other hand, he and the chief reporter of *The Inquirer* (from which most lies and scandal originate), have had a relationship stretching back years. A moment's refection, then Stride turns round and heads determinedly towards 'the street of ink'. Sometimes protocol must cede to pragmatism. This is one of those times.

Stride enters the maze of little streets, courts and alleyways leading off the Strand until he passes under a brick arch that leads to the shabby building that houses the offices of *The Inquirer*, which is situated close to the Inns of Court. He crosses the small court where a solitary gas-lamp presides over a paved courtyard where sparrows peck, cats prowl and a few trees struggle to combat the dusty decay.

Old memories surface as Stride climbs the stairs to the offices of the newspaper. He recalls other times, when he has stormed up them, filled with indignation over the spewings of Richard Dandy, then a minor reporter, always his nemesis. Most of the time, after a heated debate, the editor has acceded to his wishes and the piece has been spiked before it could do much reputational damage. Stride hopes the same procedure with be enacted on this occasion. Reaching the top of the stairs, he knocks, enters the outer office, and requests a meeting with Mr Elliot Stock, the editor, at his earliest convenience ~ as in, at once.

The secretary gives him a slightly puzzled look, then scurries into the inner sanctum. Meanwhile Stride surveys the framed posters of early editions of *The Inquirer* with distaste. It was a rag then; it is a rag now. He is mentally lining up his current argument when the door opens and a familiar and well-hated figure advances into the room.

"Well, well, if it isn't old Stride! Come to congratulate me?" Richard Dandy grins.

Stride's jaw drops open.

"Yes, you see before you the new editor of *The Inquirer* ~ the paper that speaks for the common man. And right now, the common man is not a happy man at all, I can tell you that for a pint of winkles."

"You? You are the editor? Since when?" Stride is in shock.

Dandy's grin broadens. "Since this morning. Mr Stock retired last night ~ today's first edition was his last. From now on, it's my paper, reporting the news I think people want to read about. Can I offer you a small glass of something to toast my success, Stride? I believe there is a bottle of sherry in the office left over from last night's farewell gathering."

Stride swallows hard. "No. No sherry. I have come to see the editor about your latest lies about the 'London plague'. You must retract it at once. At once, do you understand?"

Dandy perches himself on the edge of the secretary's desk and folds his arms. "Now then, Stride, let's consider the facts. Do you deny that some people have died from catching this disease ~ and before you answer, I know all about the London Hospital porter? Do you deny that bodies from the last plague pandemic have been dug up on a building site? In the light of this, do you deny that any good citizen of London going about their daily business all innocent and unprepared, might not be the next victim? Is it not the duty of a responsible news outlet to warn them? Coz from where I'm sitting, it looks like those in authority want to sweep it under the carpet and pretend it isn't happening."

Stride's back and shoulders are so rigid, they could be laid flat and used as an ironing board. "London is not in the midst of an outbreak of plague," he says between gritted teeth. "Yes, I do not deny what you have said, but that is as far as it goes. The bodies have been disposed of and nobody ... I repeat NOBODY is in any danger. To deliberately frighten people into thinking they might be the next victim is unconscionable. I demand you issue a retraction."

Dandy shakes his head. "Demand away, Stride. Makes no difference. I have it on the best authority, from an expert in the field, that there might be an outbreak any day now."

"What 'expert'?" Stride demands angrily.

"Your own police surgeon ~ Robertson, I believe he's called." Dandy fishes a notebook from his pocket, flicks through a couple of pages, then halts: "Here we are. Quote: *'He doesn't think there is any danger. Though he did say one must always consider the possibility that the event might be replicated.'* Can't get ANY clearer than that, can you? Straight from the horse's mouth, as it were."

"Mr Robertson would never speak to the likes of you!" Stride exclaims indignantly.

"I didn't say he did. I am merely quoting him. But he did say it. Got it down here in black and white. *Verbatim*, as you might say. Well, you probably wouldn't."

"You're making it up," Stride says.

Dandy leers at him. "Listen, chum. I was in a pub the other night. Group of medical students talking at the next table. Heard one of them say it. You telling me a medic would lie? Respect'ble profession like that? 'Course he wouldn't. So we, as a responsible newspaper, have a duty to the man in the street ~ let alone his wife and kiddies, to warn them. And it's no good you coming round here shouting the odds, Stride, because I know for a fact that you're no longer in charge of those so-called forces of law and order at Scotland Yard, so you have no authority there or anywhere else. And on that note, I will bid you good day. Can't sit here wasting my time. More important things to be getting on with."

And with that, the new editor slides his bulk off the desk and without a backward glance or a handshake, returns to his inner sanctum, leaving behind an ex-detective inspector who finds himself suddenly speechless and shaking with rage.

Some time later, his fury having slightly dissipated on the walk back, Stride enters Scotland Yard, where he immediately makes his way across the courtyard to the mortuary, a place he hoped he would never have to visit again. There were many aspects of his previous job that he enjoyed, sparring with Robertson was not one of them. He could never understand the police surgeon's enthusiasm for corpses and the slimy bits found inside them. As far as Stride was concerned, the nearest he preferred to be to a dead body was not at all. Plus, Robertson's domain also contained small hammers, knives, cranial saws, and strange things floating in jars.

Robertson is bent over the dissecting table when Stride enters. His eyes are focussed, his expression eager. At his side, a young, white-aproned assistant is handing gruesome-looking tools as requested. On the table is an object that once was human, but now resembles something one might encounter in a butcher's shop. Robertson glances up. Then sets down the fearsome saw he is wielding.

"My word! It's Detective Inspector Stride ~ the former detective inspector, should I more properly say. I did not think to see you patronising my humble quarters again, given your previous reluctance. *Timor mortuis conturbat me* ~ eh?"

Stride mentally adds Robertson's use of Latin expressions to the list of reasons he is glad he doesn't have to be here ever again. And yet, here he is.

"May I introduce young Master Anstruther," Robertson continues, gesturing towards the young man. "He is here to learn the finer points of postmortem dissection and diagnosis. Master Anstruther, meet the now retired Detective Inspector Stride. In his day he was one of Scotland Yard's most able investigators."

And still is, Stride thinks, eyeing the youthful assistant while various cogs whir and slot into place in his brain. "Master Anstruther, good day. Are you are finding your work here interesting? Yes, I thought so. And I expect you like to share some of your experiences with your student friends in the evenings when you finish. Maybe over a drink or two? Am I right? Yes, I imagine that to be the case.

"So, can you recall sharing the arrival of a sack full of very old bones? Maybe you also hinted where they came from? Perhaps you enjoyed scaring your friends by suggesting there could be a recurrence of the disease that caused the demise of their owners, as Mr Robertson might have said?" The student does not reply. Stride nods. "Of course, you weren't to know that there was a reporter from one of the more scandalous papers sitting close enough to hear every word of your conversation. No, you didn't know that, did you? Nor that your careless chatter would now be reported as fact in nearly every lunchtime London newspaper today. Though one might have assumed that you *did* know sharing anything that occurs in this room, outside of this room, is a breach of medical ethics."

Stride switches his gaze to the police surgeon. They have a brief exchange of significant glances. Then Robertson's mouth sets in a firm line and he swivels round to face the student.

"Mr Anstruther, you are weighed in the balance and found wanting," the police surgeon remarks drily. "Please return your outer covering, and the various objects you have helped yourself to during your brief tenure, then stand not upon the order of your going, but go at once." He nods at Stride, and without making further eye contact with the hapless medical student, picks up his saw, and returns to sawing up the human remains on the table.

Stride turns on his heel and goes back to the basement to continue with his research. There are questions that shouldn't be asked, he thinks to himself. And questions that should be. The problem arises when the questions are the same.

****

Only one question is currently being considered by Mr Henry Bruce, or to give him his correct appellation, Baron Aberdare, who has summoned the head of the Detective Division and a senior member of the board of governors of the London Hospital to his room on the first floor of the Home Office building in King Charles Street, and the question is: how to contain either the plague epidemic or the rumour of a plague epidemic.

It is past the usual hours of government business, and there are candles lit in the apartment, as Greig and Trelawney are ushered into the Home Secretary's presence by his private secretary, a thin, sallow-faced person dressed in black, who carries with him the air of a funeral mute, and a pile of documents. The room they enter is spacious and lofty. The walls are hung with portraits of eminent statesmen who have held this high office in the past, and there is a round table in the middle, groaning with a mass of papers. Henry Bruce sits at the table, his square face clean shaven, greying hair tidily curled over his ears. He observes them with a keen gaze, and gestures that they are to sit opposite him.

"Welcome, gentlemen," Bruce greets them, the lilt in his voice betraying his Welsh origins. "I have invited you here ~ and I apologise for the lateness of the hour, but I have been in the House or in meetings all day, because before I take any formal action, I need you to appraise me of all of the facts. We are staring a possible human catastrophe in the face, gentlemen, one that is unprecedented in modern times, and it behoves us all to act swiftly, but at the same time to act responsibly. Sir Charles, may I turn to you first, and will you excuse me if I make notes while you speak."

The private secretary discreetly places a sheet of foolscap writing paper, a pen, and some blotting paper in front of the Home Secretary, then makes a brief bow and leaves the room, closing the door quietly behind him. The Home Secretary picks up the pen and looks at Trelawney, indicting with a nod that he should start speaking.

Trelawney clears his throat awkwardly. Pauses, then outlines the course of events from the discovery of the young Irish labourer's body outside the hospital, to the death of the elderly porter. He touches, in passing, on his regret at not making the deaths official, but does not mention the bruising earlier encounter with Richard Dandy and his press colleagues. "I have, of course, tended my resignation to the hospital board," he finishes lamely.

Henry Bruce glances up at him. "Yes, I think in the circumstances that is the correct thing to do," he says evenly. "Now, chief inspector, I gather that you have managed to find the source of the contagion."

Greig has taken the opportunity to make his own notes, in anticipation of this meeting. Now he reads from them, putting in detail, dates, and actions. He is relieved to see Bruce nodding in agreement every now and then.

"Thank you, chief inspector. That was very clear and most helpful. The positives we can take from it are that there have been no further deaths ~ as far as we know, and the source of the outbreak has been destroyed." He pauses. "Even so, I fear it may be too late. I refer you to the headlines in some of the less reputable newspapers ~ headlines which have been repeated and augmented in the evening editions. I do not know whether either of you are aware of the lurid stories circulating, but from my experience, the maxim 'no smoke without fire' inevitably follows such assertions. We may not be in the throes of a plague epidemic, thank God, gentlemen, but we are on the cusp of a full-blown public panic. People will be very frightened, even though there is nothing to fear, and when people are frightened, they are not logical in their behaviour."

"You cannot allow cheap newspapers to spread lies and distortions!" Trelawney huffs.

"Had we known from the beginning what was happening, we might have been able to take steps to stop them," Bruce observes tartly. "As it is, it is too late now, and we will be reduced to fighting a rear-guard action to mitigate the situation. I am dining later with Delane, the editor of *The Times*. I propose to brief him on our discussion and ask him to counter the misinformation with headlines and articles promoting the actual facts. He is sympathetic to the Liberal cause and his newspaper has a good reputation with the better class of reading public."

"Do you think that will be enough, though?" Greig asks.

The Home Secretary brings the tips of his fingers together and leans his chin meditatively upon them. "I very much doubt it, chief inspector. I think we are in for a turbulent few weeks, and we need to be prepared for whatever happens. Until something 'better' takes the fancy of the popular press, that is. I suggest you alert your men to the possibility of street disturbances and civil disorder. Best to be ready in advance. Now, if you would both excuse me, I should like to spend some time going over my notes and thinking through what I shall say before my evening meeting. I intend to hold a full Cabinet meeting first thing tomorrow morning where we will discuss the problem and work out a strategy. I shall, of course, keep you informed."

Greig rises. As if by magic, the door opens, and the private secretary appears. Greig hurries straight off; he has no desire to listen to Trelawney's litany of self-pity. He makes his way to the Horse Guards cab rank where he picks up a hansom, directing the driver to take him back to St John's Wood. All the way home, the words 'turbulent few weeks' ring ominously in his ears.

****

Meanwhile, elsewhere in the city, within the private quarters of Jasper and Avice Broxton, questions of a different nature are being considered. We find the uxorious pair seated in Avice's sitting room, away from the listening ears of servants and their daughter Johanna. The door is closed, the curtains drawn, shutting out the night. The gas-lamp is turned down low, filling the room with shadows. The topic under discussion is the imminent arrival of the Broxton heiress. It involves a lot of hissed fury on the part of Jasper Broxton, whose natural inclination to shout and throw china has to be supressed for the sake of secrecy.

"I don't care what the lawyer fellow says, damn him: this girl, this by-blow of some inappropriate liaison, this ditch drab of a child cannot be allowed to pass herself off as a Broxton," Jasper Broxton snarls (quietly) bringing his clenched fist down upon the arm of the small spoon-back chair. "I simply will not allow it! I will not let the ancient name of Broxton be dragged into the gutter by that ugly scheming spinster cousin of mine and her milksop of a sister!"

"What I do not understand," Avice murmurs, frowning, "is how they think the child could possibly be accepted in any good society. It is beyond me."

"The whole thing is a total disgrace," Jasper Broxton grips the arms of the chair as if he is trying to strangle the life out of it. "I am prepared to be as modern as the next man ~ after all we live in an enlightened age, but A CHILD BORN OUT OF WEDLOCK? A LITTLE BASTARD?"

Avice puts her finger to her lips. "Pas devant les domestiques," she mouths. "I have had another letter from the maid," she continues, going to her dressing table and opening a drawer. "It came this afternoon. I have not opened it as I thought it prudent to wait for your return." She proffers the cheap envelope to her better half, who almost snatches it from her hand. He rips it open, extracts the sheet of flimsy writing paper and reads the contents.

"Faugh!" he mutters. "So that's how it's going to be, is it? Well, we shall see. Oh yes, we shall indeed see about that."

"May I please read my letter?" Avice remarks huffily.

Broxton holds it out. She studies the ill-spelled lines that inform her that the child, called Ruth, will be arriving on Thursday, and a lavishly furnished bedroom is being prepared for her. The staff have been instructed to address her as Miss Broxton or Miss Ruth, and she is to be treated with every courtesy and respect, as befits her new status.

Avice's face falls. "And so, the lawyer says there is nothing we can do?"

"There is plenty we can do," Broxton counters. "You will write to the maid tomorrow and ask her to keep a close eye on the girl. I want to know every detail." He laughs harshly. "Ruth indeed? Well, we are going to be 'ruthless' in removing this cuckoo from our nest!"

Crouched on the landing, wrapped in a shawl, Johanna Broxton listens to her parents trying to talk quietly. She has learned over the years that whenever they retire to her mama's sitting room, it is to discuss something that they do not want her to hear. Frequently, the conversation is about her ~ some fault, some flaw or failing, and the remedy, which will be applied without consultation.

Since this business of the discovered heiress, however, less attention has been paid to her scrapes and misdemeanours, for which she is almost grateful. Her complete failure to recite that dreadful poem has passed without comment or punishment. The letter she was given to take home to her parents lingers at the bottom of her schoolbag, where it is becoming gradually ink stained and encrumbed.

Johanna Broxton hugs her knees. Part of her is angry that all the wonderful promises she'd been made, look like coming to nought. Part of her is delighted that her parents are so furious with someone who isn't her. She grins in the shadowy darkness at her father's appalling pun. She has been pretty ruthless over the past few days herself, as the two charity brats could testify. Always pinch, slap, or kick them where the bruises won't show ~ that's what Shedleigh taught her. It's actually one of the very few lessons she has managed to master to perfection.

****

Under a wild moon and restless clouds, London sleeps. Gas lamps throw their fitful and garish lustre upon brightly illuminated shop windows. The streets are quiet. The main thoroughfares, which seem to stretch to infinity, are lit up like lines of brilliant fire, redrawing the map of the city into alternating lines of light and dark, into unlit alleys and brightly lit squares, touching abandoned houses and half-built ones alike.

And as dawn slowly breaks over the city, and the milk carts, coaches, wagons, and workers stir into life, rumour runs through the streets, fleet of foot, swift, silent and invisible to the nightwatchman and the patrolling constable. By morning, the rumour has settled itself in, got its feet under the table and made itself at home.

Jack Cully, making his way to work in the company of his daughter Violet is the first to notice its presence. He observes, to his astonishment, that some people have covered their faces with scarves, or handkerchiefs. A few are wearing cardboard masks, such as might be donned at some Roman Carnival. These individuals are taking great care not to walk too close to other pedestrians on the footway, sometimes choosing to risk their lives by venturing into the actual road, where they are in great danger from passing wheel and hoof.

From initial puzzlement, Cully moves swiftly to the realization that this is the outcome of the dramatic headlines in yesterday's newspapers. Luckily, Violet is far too preoccupied with her upcoming day to observe the peculiar behaviour of her fellow commuters. Cully sees her to 'their' corner, then hurries on his way. A strategy has to be put in place before the whole city descends into madness and chaos.

As he crosses Covent Garden piazza, he sees his former boss in earnest conversation with the elderly couple running the corner coffee stall. Drawing nearer, he realises it is more in the nature of a dispute than a conversation. Stride spots him and waves him over to join him. "Tell them, Jack!" he commands.

"What do you need me to tell them?" Cully asks.

"Tell them there is no plague in London. That they can let me have my usual coffee in a mug quite safely."

"See, we ain't so sure, sir," the elderly man shakes his head. "Way we heard it, you can catch it from crockery. So we ain't doing drinks no more, only bread and butter. Till the plague goes."

"Or till we goes," his wife adds. "I told you, Henry: our Meg says we can stay with her in the countryside. It's safe out there. No plague."

"Well, old girl, it's summat to fink about. Don't want to end our days being frown into a pit."

Jack Cully puts out a comforting arm. The old man draws back, his face fearful.

"What can I tell you both to reassure you?" Cully says gently. "There is no plague, as my colleague says. It is just a story being bandied about by some unscrupulous journalists to sell copies of their newspapers. You shouldn't believe anything you read; the stories are nearly always lies or exaggeration."

"So there weren't never no dead bodies then, is that what you're saying?"

Honesty compels Cully to say, "Yes, a few unfortunate people did catch it and die, but they were the only ones. And there is no plague now. None. It has been dealt with."

The old couple exchange uncertain glances. "We'd like to believe you, sir. Honest we would. And Mr Stride, but we read it in the newspapers, you see. And our neighbours are packing up their house and leaving. So if it's all the same to you both, better safe than sorry. Bread and butter? On the house?"

Feeling that Stride is about to resume remonstrating with the couple, Cully takes him firmly by the arm and steers him towards Scotland Yard. "I am sure your wise advice will be appreciated elsewhere today," he says. They enter the building together, to be greeted by the desk constable "Mr Greig wants to see all detectives in his office at once," he says. Stride hesitates, but Cully still has hold of his arm. "I definitely think you should come to the meeting," he says. "You may have insights on how to deal with this." Then, seeing the reluctant expression on Stride's face, "I insist. This isn't a time for scruples. On anybody's behalf."

The head of Scotland Yard's Detective Division occupies an office (Stride's former office) that could comfortably accommodate five men. Thus, when Stride and Cully arrive, there are detectives massing by the open door and spilling into the corridor. Word having spread that 'something pretty important is afoot', there are also various lower ranks lurking on the perimeter. The two men engineer their way to the back of the room and squeeze themselves into a space by the wall opposite the desk. Stride recollects it as the wall he used to throw things at, when angry or upset.

Upon their arrival, Lachlan Greig rises from behind the desk and advances to stand in front of it. He looks utterly exhausted, pale, with dark shadows under his eyes (a combination of the current crisis and the ongoing teething problems of Master Greig).

"Gentlemen," Greig begins. "I have summoned you all here because we are, as some of you know, in the midst of one of the greatest crises to hit the city since the cholera outbreak of 1853. You will have read in some of the more unscrupulous and scandal-rid newspapers that there is an epidemic of plague. Some of you may well have been approached by members of the public anxious about their own safety.

"I am now in a position to state categorically and for any future reference that there is NO epidemic. An old plague pit was accidentally opened on one of the many excavations taking place to install the new sewerage system. One unfortunate workman succumbed to the fatal disease, along with the porter who took in his body at the London Hospital. Three elderly derelicts working in the area of the pit also succumbed. The bodies have been quickly and effectively disposed of. All this happened several weeks ago. Since then, there have been no deaths in the city from plague. None whatsoever.

"However, despite attempts to keep events away from the public arena, a few newspaper men discovered what occurred and are now hellbent on creating chaos, fear, and panic amongst our citizens. They must be stopped, and this is why I have called you all into my office. Each of you heads up a team of men, who regularly patrol the streets day and night and know their neighbourhoods. I ask you to relay to them the simple message that there is no plague in London, and order them to spread that same message to every individual, business, family, church congregation, or household they come into contact with. Exactly the same message is being passed to all officers, via their superintendents, in all nineteen Metropolitan police divisions, so that we all say the same thing.

"You may have to repeat the message many times; you may find people will argue with you, or claim they know better, but I urge you not to be swayed or diverted. Last night I met with the Home Secretary, and have his word that Parliament will support our endeavours to close this story before it runs out of control. Any individual who has further questions at any time in the future, please come and discuss it with me. Do not talk to members of the press under any circumstances ~ that is an order, and I will punish severely the man of whatever rank who disobeys it. That is all I wish to say to you. Please now go about your daily duties and thank you for attending this meeting."

As the senior officers disperse, Stride remains where he is. He wants to tell Greig that their old foe Richard Dandy is now the editor of their worst nightmare *The Inquirer* and impress upon him that although he went to try to dissuade him from printing his dangerous lies, he, Stride, has no intention of interfering in the investigation. Cully touches his shoulder lightly. "Another time," he murmurs. "I think he has enough to cope with." Stride stares across at Greig. He has moved back behind his desk and is sitting, arms folded, head down, staring at absolutely nothing. It is a stance Stride recognises only too well from his time in charge. "Maybe you are right, another time," he agrees, following Jack Cully out of the room.

Out in the corridor, Stride updates Cully with the news about Richard Dandy, both deciding that at least he won't be prowling the streets making their lives even more complicated. Then Stride makes his way to the basement, where he attempts to get to grips with another boxful of case files. But without his usual dose of caffeine, his mind wanders. Eventually, he gives up the unequal struggle and sets off in search of some liquid stimulant.

Stride's feet carry him automatically towards his favourite watering hole: the booth at the back of Sally's chop-house. Here he hopes to find refreshment, both physical and intellectual. The meeting in Greig's office was a poignant reminder that he no longer has any role, place, or status at Scotland Yard.

Reaching his destination, Stride is very surprised to find the door locked ~ an almost unheard-of event. Even when Sally was forced by his wife to take a few days off, he had arranged an (inadequate) replacement. Stride hammers on the door with his fist until the eponymous owner arrives on the other side and the door is opened a crack.

"Luncheon?" Stride says hopefully, attempting to insert himself into the small opening.

Sally eyes him up and down carefully. "You got any symptoms, Mr Stride?"

"Yes: I'm hungry and I need a plate of your stewed mutton and a glass of ale. What's going on, Sally? Surely you haven't fallen for these idiotic rumours about a plague epidemic? I thought you were more sensible than to believe any old rubbish you read in the newspapers."

Sally folds his massive arms over his food-stained apron. "Got it on the best orfority, Mr Stride. Falling like ninepins along the Commercial Road. Fine in the morning, dead by the evening."

"Rubbish!" Stride exclaims. "Absolute rubbish! If that were so, we'd know about it at Scotland Yard. Now, you let me in and serve me my luncheon and we'll hear no more about plagues, you understand?"

There is a long pause while mine host works on his options. Stride can almost hear the cogs whirring away in Sally's brain. Finally, "Werll ... I dunno, Mr Stride," Sally says, screwing up his face. "Seems it's a bit of a dry lemon, as they say. If I lets you in, I'll have to open up, and if I open up, who knows who might walk in orf the street and what they might bring in wiv them, if you see what I mean. Gotta think of the wife and kids. So, if it's all the same to you, I ain't going to open up, not just yet. No offence. There's the Black Boy just round the corner. You could try there." And with this, Sally closes the door once more and attaches the chain, leaving an astonished Stride to make his way to the Black Boy, an inferior, malodorous hostelry with tobacco-stained walls, a sulky barmaid, and a reputation of serving meat of dubious provenance and watered-down beer.

After an unsatisfactory meal for which he is sure he has been overcharged, Stride returns to Scotland Yard. He hears the newsvendors shouting the midday headlines. People hurry past, their faces drawn and anxious, some have fashioned masks from pieces of cloth or cardboard. He sees shops with their shutters down and 'Closed until further notice' signs pinned to the doors. It is like living in a parallel city.

On his return, he spies a liveried manservant standing by the front desk. The constable manning the desk is looking harried. He meets Stride's eye over the top of the servant's head and fires off a desperate look. Stride goes over.

"Yes?" he inquires.

"This man says his master wants to talk to someone in charge," the constable says. "I've told him they are all busy or out of the building."

The manservant turns to face Stride. "My master, the noble Marquis of Losiberne and Staines, is waiting in his carriage," he says loftily, eying Stride with distaste. "He has been waiting for some time."

"Has he now?" Stride says grimly. "Then we'd better go and talk to him, hadn't we?"

Stride follows the supercilious manservant back out into the street, and then round the corner, where a large, old-fashioned, shiny black barouche awaits. There is another matching footman sitting on the high box seat and inside, glaring out at the passing populace, a bald, elderly, whiskery-chinned man, yellow of hue and irate of eye, wearing a black frock coat, and a high white cravat fastened with a diamond pin. Seeing his servant reappearing, his face compresses into an expression of rage.

Stride feels his spirits rise. He has been spoiling for a fight ever since he was deprived of his morning's dose of caffeine. He deliberately slows his pace until he comes alongside the carriage. Then he waits. No formal bow. No acknowledgement that he is in the presence of one of 'his betters'. Stride was educated on the Pavement School of Life where he learned to thoroughly despise the aristocracy, the upper classes and the parvenues who thought they were superior to the rest of the populace. And superior in all respects to him. At some point in every encounter he has ever had throughout his whole career in the police force, he is always informed that he is a public servant, the aristocrat pays his salary and is a close friend of the Prime Minister.

Man and marquis eye each other silently. Stride lets the silence develop. He is good at this, he thinks. He has forgotten how much he enjoys making an opponent feel uncomfortable. Eventually, the marquis speaks. "Now, look here, my good man. This damned plague outbreak business. What are you doin' to stop it? Why aren't all these people bein' locked up in their houses instead of bein' allowed to tramp the streets spreadin' contagion everywhere they go? It's not good enough, damned if it ain't!"

"I am sorry that you feel inconvenienced," Stride says, etching every word with acid. "What exactly would you like me to do?"

The marquis waves a black-gloved hand vaguely in the direction of passers-by. "Get them orf the streets. Good God, man, it shouldn't be beyond your ability!"

"And how are they supposed to earn their daily bread if they can't work? Or eat it if they can't visit the shops that sell it? You want people to starve, I suppose?"

The marquis glares at him. "Insolence will get you nowhere," he growls between yellowing teeth. Stride waits for the inevitable. "You should bear in mind that you are a mere public servant. I pay your salary. And where are your Bills of Mortality? I demand to see one."

"Certainly." Stride whistles to the footman. "Go and ask whoever is on duty on the front desk to bring me a piece of paper. Quick as you can." The footman, fleet of foot, disappears round the corner. Stride inserts his thumbs into his waistcoat pocket and admires the brickwork. He can almost feel the steam coming from the barouche parked behind his back. When the footman returns, now somewhat out of breath, Stride produces a pencil, writes on the piece of paper in capital letters, then gives it to the footman to hand to the marquis.

"What is this?" the aristocrat says, waving the paper in the air.

"Please read it. I believe it is headed: Plague Bill of Mortality and dated today."

"There's nothing written there."

"Yes. That's because nobody has died. Of plague. Because there is no plague. So there are no deaths from it. Now if you'll excuse me, I have business to attend to."

Stride spins round and walks away, without a farewell. Behind him, the words "How dare you turn your back on me. I will report your insolence. Oh yes, indeed. I know the Prime Minister, you know," float into the ether. He ignores them.

Once out of sight of the noble marquis, Stride slows. A thought has suddenly struck him. If all the police offices in the city regularly post Bills of Mortality, with no deaths noted, it might, over time, convince the populace that there is no plague. He decides to suggest the idea to Lachlan Greig, once he has worked out a way to do it that doesn't look as if he is trying to elbow his way back in. Stride enters the building. The desk constable greets him. He heads for the basement. On the way down he meets one of his old team, who expresses his great pleasure at seeing him again. It is almost like old times. Except it isn't.

****

London panics. The city starts imperceptibly changing. Once there is a doubt, there is no doubt. The rich seal off their big tree-lined squares and set watchmen in boxes at each entry point to keep out the possibly infected. Many quit the city altogether and make for their country houses or temporarily rent places elsewhere. Others refuse to leave, declaring they will not run away like those fleeing cowards, but will stay to the bitter end. Heroes in the face of adversity.

Doctors' surgeries and hospital waiting rooms start filling up with members of the public who imagine they have caught the plague. Nobody has any idea what to look for, so a sneeze, a spot, a boil, a headache, or a weakness in any limbs suddenly becomes cause for concern. The talk in the street is all of pills, potions, salves, ointments. Astrologers, alchemists, soothsayers, fortune tellers, card readers, table turners, magi and holy men of extremely dubious provenance suddenly find themselves in great demand, their nostrums swallowed, their strictures read avidly, their coffers filling.

Signs and wonders, omens and portents are widely reported and mulled over by those who hold such things as deeply significant. Ghosts are seen in the street, parading bold as brass. They lean against doorposts, they appear at windows, they skulk in shadows, bare-boned outlines in the darkness of alleyways. A two-headed fish is caught upriver, allegedly singing doleful songs as it is landed. Church bells ring without anybody's help and candles ignite spontaneously. A woman gives birth to a child with the face of a pig. All these are held as true facts, evidence that the world has become strange and unpredictable, that the pestilence has disturbed the natural order of things and are seized upon eagerly by the many and various strange sects that inhabit the corners and crevices of the mainstream religious community.

Here is one such: The Truly Sanctified Disciples of God's Ultimate Revelation, who meet every Tuesday evening above a local pie and mash shop to listen to the Word interpreted to them through the preaching of Brother Elias Zadok, who used to be a master printer until the Lord's Holy Spirit anointed him one afternoon, shortly after being accidentally hit on the head by a tray of letters.

Prior to the plague scare, the Sanctified were lucky if they got half a dozen members turning up. Now, their numbers have risen incrementally to over thirty and more seats have had to be sourced from divers places. Tonight, their numbers have increased even more, though due to the fear of infection, everybody is sitting as far away from their neighbour as they can, which is causing access problems for late arrivals.

After twenty minutes of earnest hymn singing, Brother Zadok mounts the wooden fish crate that stands in for a pulpit. He is a lean man in his early fifties, his hair long and straggly, his beard uncombed, and profuse. He cultivates the Old Testament prophet look and customarily dresses in a black robe, with a medallion bearing a strange device of a quasi-religious nature (his own design). He glances slowly round the waiting congregation and raises a hand. Silence falls. He closes his eyes, rocks gently back and forth. Then, reaching into a capacious coat pocket, he extracts something, which he holds out to the congregants in a suitably dramatic manner.

"What, my brothers and sisters is this?" he intones in a low, intense voice.

"It's a potato," comes a voice from the back row.

"Look more closely, brethren. I ask you once more: what is this?"

"It's still a potato."

Brother Zadok recognises the voice as coming from one of the 'new' disciples. He sends him a withering look. "To some unenlightened people, it *may* look like a potato ~ but if you see with the opened eyes of the enlightened, it bears on one side the face of Our Lord Himself."

A gasp runs round the room. Swelling visibly Brother Zadok fixes his gaze a few feet above the heads of his acolytes, all the better to command their full and undivided attention. Sure enough, everyone dutifully looks up. "THIS is a sign, brethren," he intones in a sepulchral voice, waving the holy potato.

"It is a message from On High. God has communicated with us. We must go out into the highways and byways of this wicked city ... this Babylon, this Whore, and proclaim the end of the world is at hand. For is it not written: there will come upon the land plagues and pestilence? It is written indeed! And hath not the city been stricken with plague? It hath! Woe, Woe, Oh Babylon, your doom has come! Your destruction is at Hand! For the Lord has weighed you in the balance and found you Wanting!"

The sound of communal indrawing breath follows this pronouncement. As well it might. But before Brother Zadok can resume speaking, another voice from the back of the room cautiously asks: "If it is the end of the world ~ what is going to happen to the likes of us? Will we perish along with the whores? Coz I just got my winter cabbages planted out and it seems a shame I won't be here to harvest them."

Brother Zadok sighs and rolls his eyes heavenwards. Always the same. When he was working as a printer, there was always some fussy customer who quibbled about the price. Or the shape of the letter R. Or that there seemed to be three page fours. If he had his way, the whole lot of them would burn in eternal hellfire. He swivels round and fixes his basilisk gaze upon the hapless disciple. Who cowers.

"The Lord has spoken," Brother Zadok declaims. "He has sent us the signs. BUT," he pauses, for emphasis, "He is a God big with mercy and he MIGHT, if we obey his will, spare us from the terrors that are to come. There are pamphlets at the back of the room. I expect everybody to take some and hand them to the SINNERS they meet. This is HIS will. NO mercy, however, will be extended to the citizens of Babylon, to those dressed in fine linen, purple and scarlet, for Lo ~ they will suffer torture and grief. They will drink of the cup filled with the wine of His Fury and Wrath!"

There follows another twenty minutes of ranting on very similar lines, but, gentle reader, we will leave at this point, and seek an elsewhere to be.

****

And here we are, in Kilburn High Street, with its chandlers' shops where tea and sugar are sold by the farthings-worth and where you can also purchase oil, candles, mops, Dutch brooms, shovels, kettles, pots, pans, nails and treacle. Here are cook-shops with puddings galore, their windows foggy with steam. Here is the shop that sells second-hand goods of all kinds, next door to the pawn broker's. Here is the butcher, the baker and the barber, the pharmacist, the tailor, and the tavern. And here is Beech's coffee-shop, where a cup of something that calls itself coffee and a slice of damp cake can be purchased for a penny each.

It is raining, which is driving the local street vendors indoors. Here are three of them, Walt, Bobs and Charlie, flash costers all, wearing velveteen coats set off with numerous brass, pearl and carved bone buttons. They have cord trousers and good stout boots, their silk neckcloths tied in fancy knots round their throats. Charlie's girl, who at eighteen is a few years older than Charlie, has just joined them, her crushed bonnet dripping water down her bright shawl and heavy cotton print dress.

"My, it's wet out vere," she says, sliding into a seat next to her man. "Giss a piecer cake, Charlie, I'm fair starved."

Some cake is passed across. Charlie's girl gobbles it down gratefully. "Watchoo talkin' abaht ven?" she asks, wiping her mouth on her shawl.

"If you MUST know, we was discussing this plague," Charlie says. "There's money to be made aht of it and I was telling the boys that I know how."

His girl, who works in a frowsty attic as a stitcher of shirts, tosses her curls and shudders. "Don't talk to ME abaht plague. S'all I hears day in day out: who's got it, who's not got it. Who's dyin', who's dead. On and on, so's at the ender the day, I leaves wiv me head banging."

Charlie cuffs her affectionately on the shoulder. "One day soon, you won't haveter stitch stitch away ev'ry hour God sends. If'n my scheme comes orff, you'll have yer own little set of rooms, where you can sit all day long wiv yer feet on the fender, drinkin' tea if yer wants."

He turns to the others. "So this is the plan. I got good few reg'lars up West now ~ folks in the h'aristocratic line, you might say. I know them and they knows me. Then there's all the pretty ladies in their nice villas up Maida Vale way, they like their fresh fruit and veggies and they pay well too. I know a man who can get his hands on some nice plump birds, no questions asked. So here's the plan: while everyone's too scared to leave their houses in case they catch this plague, and the shops is not making deliv'ries, we go round and offer to buy whatever they want: milk, bread, meat, green stuff. They leave us a list ~ we leave them the goods. We charge a fair price, but with a bit added on coz we're delivering personally to their door."

"Sounds good," Walt says. "I'm in."

"You'll need to gussy up your pony and trap a bit," Charlie says. "These folks ain't yer usual mob. We got to put on a bit of a show. Make them feel we ain't ordin'ry street costers."

"I'll get to work on Daisy with a brush and a bit of ribbon soon as the rain eases orf," Walt nods. "You won't reckernise her."

"What about me?" Bobs asks. "I only got the old moke and a barrow."

Charlie sits back and grins affably at his comrade in the street retail trade. "I got a special job for you, Bobs. You will be selling orf anything we got left. Plenty of people still wanter buy food after work, 'specially as most of the grocers and cook shops are closing early now. Then you'll take your barrow down the market first light and buy what we need for the next day."

"And when do I sleep?" Bobs asks plaintively.

Charlie laughs harshly. "When you're dead," he says shortly. "What's sleep when we got money to make." He glances out of the grimy coffee shop window. "Rain's clearing. Time to push orf. Them apples ain't going to sell themselves." He hauls himself to his feet, glances down. "Might be 'ome late ternight, me gal. Gotta a lotta doors to knock on. Don't wait up."

Meanwhile, in the wider world of the great city, mitigating strategies continue to be put in place. The 'better' newspapers stick strictly to the official line: there is no plague outbreak. There are no deaths in the city. They cite reports from local cemeteries and funeral parlours, who have received no bodies. They quote the 'Plague Mortality Bills' now posted daily outside every police office, which continue to contain no names. The rest of the cheaper papers find ever more lurid and improbable stories to scare their readership witless.

The Home Secretary, true to his word, strenuously denies the rumours in a series of well-written articles, and issues a request that all food shops and eateries remain open, so that the ordinary clerk and workman can refresh himself, and his wife and family be fed.

The Prime Minister gives him his full public support and MPs of all stripes can be seen confidently coming and going, entering their clubs, and walking around the streets of Westminster in a completely normal manner. Various hospitals publish positive stories of absolutely no plague admissions whatsoever to their wards. Everyone in authority crosses their fingers and hopes that something else will quickly emerge to distract from the story.

Let us now step away from the locked doors, the lowered blinds, the masked citizens and the many night-time 'Bring out your Dead' carts that are filled with defunct dogs, cats, general detritus and the odd songbird. Let us revisit the spacious if decaying Regent's Park townhouse of the Broxton family, who have not decamped to other pastures principally because they haven't got an anywhere to decamp to that wouldn't end up costing them money. Plus, Jasper Broxton does not believe, like many of his ilk, that he will ever catch anything that the readers of the lower-class penny papers might get. He may know nothing whatsoever about the nature, biology and spread of disease, but he is pretty convinced it doesn't spread socially upwards.

Today, he is hiding behind a copy of *The Times* as it stops him having to make polite breakfast conversation with his wife and daughter. Not that the latter indulges in polite conversation. Or any conversation. Broxton thinks back to the days when little Johanna's mud-coloured eyes would light up with joy when 'dear Papa' returned from work. How she would stumble down the stairs from the nursery on her chubby legs (they lived in a smaller house in those poorer times) and fling herself at his legs in joyous rapture. Now he is lucky if he gets more than a snarl and a look of contempt.

As for Shedleigh ~ his boyish pranks and pert responses are now reduced to a brief occasional letter home, which bears all the hallmarks of the writer being sat down and forced to compose a few miserable paragraphs to satisfy the people who pay his school fees, and which always ends with a request to send a cake and 'subs' as he is in dire need of them. Broxton lets Avice deal with these requests.

Broxton sips his lukewarm coffee, and studies the stock market pages, noting which company shares are going up. Building and construction firms seem to be holding their own. He feels a small sense of triumph that he has lately invested a goodly chunk of his (his clients') money in one, albeit only a two-man operation, but everybody has to start from somewhere, he reminds himself. Later, he is meeting with the owners of Ackroyd and Guskett in their office close to Farringdon underground station. The meeting is at his request: he has written to them to expect him first thing. Just a formality, the big investment has already been transferred from his bank to their bank a while ago, but he has had no acknowledgement of the money nor any contact with them and now he wants to hear about their future plans, in particular the large contract they have hinted they are about to win, for despite mitigating strategies being put in place, Broxton is still being pursued by a few persistent creditors, who need fobbing off on a temporary basis.

Jasper Broxton finishes his breakfast, folds the paper, bestows a basilisk glance round the table, and rises from his seat, indicating to the parlour maid that she can clear the breakfast things. "I shall be dining at my Club," he tells Avice shortly. It is shorthand for something else, which she suspects, but as yet has no proof.

Broxton goes into the hall, receives his top hat, which for once has been properly brushed, slides his arms into his overcoat and leaves. He walks briskly towards Farringdon, mentally planning his day: first this upcoming meeting, luncheon at one of the better and still open eating houses in Covent Garden, then dealing with correspondence, and finishing with a cosy little dinner in Maida Vale with the delightful Dulcie, who, unlike his wife, provides tasty meals, dresses attractively, and always appreciates his company, never greeting him with a scowl and a litany of complaints and demands for money he does not possess.

Arriving at Farringdon Road, Broxton weaves his way through the workers streaming out from the underground station. He checks the business card in his wallet for the number of the building he seeks, eventually reaching it: a slightly worse-for-wear three-storey brick edifice, with the names of the businesses occupying the property listed by the front door. He scans the board. There is no business called Ackroyd & Guskett listed thereupon. Puzzled, Broxton gains entrance by ringing the bell, eventually raising a man in a brown overall whom he assumes to be some sort of caretaker. The man informs him that the gentlemen he seeks no longer rent offices here, having closed down their business unexpectedly and no, he doesn't know where they have gone, none of his affair, but if he manages to find them, the owner of the building is pursuing them for unpaid rent and would be grateful for any information as to their current whereabouts.

Jasper Broxton is utterly taken aback. For some moments he just stands outside the building, staring in puzzled disbelief at the list of occupants, while the implications of what has happened slowly sink into his subconscious. This is the only address he has for Ackroyd & Guskett. If they have had to move premises, he has no way of finding them. And hot on this thought comes the dawning and horrific one: if he cannot trace them, then he has no way of knowing where and what has happened to his investment. Nor of getting back a single farthing of it.

****

So where are the two contractors Edward Ackroyd and Anton Guskett? To answer this question, one must first travel back in time, to when we last left the two men standing outside Scotland Yard, where, after a gruelling interrogation by Detectives Greig and Cully, and two inspectors from H Division (Whitechapel), they had been allowed to leave, on certain conditions. There on the footway, they had parted company, with Edward Ackroyd walking off in one direction, after pointedly refusing to agree with his partner's jaunty assertion that, one way or the other, they had got off lightly.

While Guskett returns to the site to chivvy the workmen, Ackroyd carries on walking, aimlessly at first, his mind a whirlpool of conflicting thoughts, until eventually his footsteps take him to Hungerford Suspension Bridge, where after paying the toll, he spends some time watching passengers embark and disembark from the steamboats. They all seem to have a purpose, a somewhere that awaits their arrival. Their faces look forward, their steps have intent, and their expressions are hopeful. Or so it seems to him.

Time passes. Then Ackroyd decides to return to his hotel room, as it has started raining solidly. All day long he has not eaten a bite. All day long he has tried to silence the terrible words that have been rolling like thunder around his brain: *"YOU might possibly have just unleashed upon them one of the deadliest plagues ever to be seen in this country!"* He has tried, but he cannot. He feels as if there are fingers everywhere pointing at him. People he passes are whispering accusations. He also recalls how Guskett attempted to shift all the blame onto his shoulders. Then he remembers the skull. And the black cat.

Slowly, as his mind starts to break down, and reality retreats to a farther shore, Ackroyd comes to a decision. He calls for paper and pen and when they are brought to him, he begins writing. First, a brief letter to his housekeeper at his house in St Albans, informing her where his Will is to be found and expressing gratitude for her many years of excellent service. He seals that letter and sets it aside. Now he takes up his pen and writes to his erstwhile business partner, a diatribe of recrimination and bitterness, filling two sides of closely written paper. After a while, exhausted and weeping, he seals the letter, goes down to the lobby and asks the clerk at the desk to post both letters for him.

It is now dusk. Edward Ackroyd returns to his room, puts on his topcoat and quits the hotel for the last time. The lamps in the street outside glow softly. The city is slowly morphing into its dreamlike night-time existence. Lights gleam in shop windows. Horse-drawn omnibuses and cabs roll by in a never-ending stream. Groups of people on their way to their night's entertainment rush past him, their faces hectic and flushed in the gaslight. He sees a chemist shop, its bottles of crimson, violet and green throwing blurred patterns of colour across the street. Ackroyd enters, makes a purchase, then leaves. The pavements glitter from the day's rain, the puddles picked out in lamplight.

He walks the short distance to the park. He finds a convenient bench, sits down and uncorks the bottle.

Throwing back his head, he downs the contents in one swallow, the liquid coursing through him like molten lava. He remains for a while, listening to the rustles and groans of homeless sleepers all around him, punctuated by the hooting of owls in the distance. Eventually, he staggers to his feet and sets off determinedly towards the river.

Reaching a narrow ledge under one of the bridge arches, Ackroyd slumps against the damp brick wall. The city gushes over him. Perhaps it is frightening, perhaps beautiful, he no longer knows or cares. He is here and not at the same time. He crawls towards the edge. The water is slapping rhythmically against the pillars. He stares down into its inky blackness, closes his eyes and falls, letting the river take him into its embrace, enfolding him to itself, washing away all memory of the troublesome world as it bears him off swiftly to a place of silence and peace.

****

Next morning, Anton Guskett, having spent the whole night in the arms of Morpheus and a woman called Fleurette who speaks with a French accent but actually comes from Poplar, calls in at the hotel to collect his business partner so that they can fulfil the requirements of the Metropolitan Police that they check in daily.

To his surprise, he is informed by the desk porter that Mr Ackroyd went out the night before, but according to the chamber maid, has not returned as his bed has not been slept in. Guskett sticks a nose round the door of the breakfast room, but there is no sign of his colleague. Guskett is perplexed. He is pretty sure Ackroyd would not have spent a night on the town, as he is abstemious and fastidious by inclination. He is also a great breakfaster. It is therefore a puzzle. He decides he might as well report to the nearest police station himself, before heading to the building site to supervise the newly acquired men.

On arrival, he is relieved to find everything proceeding apace and in good order, with the recently installed foreman driving the newly-hired workmen at a cracking pace, but still no sign of Ackroyd, who fails to put in an appearance for the rest of the day. This is unusual and requires an explanation. The problem is solved when Anton Guskett returns home to find the letter. Having perused its contents, he spends the rest of the evening making plans, and first thing next morning he goes to their bank with a note signed by himself and Ackroyd (he has copied the signature from the letter) requesting the entire contents of their account to be handed over to him in notes, and the account closed.

Later that afternoon, a man in a long dark overcoat, collar pulled up, hat pulled down, and carrying a battered leather travelling bag, enters the Plume of Feathers, an inn close to Tower Wharf. Giving his name as Gerald Smith, he books a bed for the night. Next morning at first light, the man boards a steamboat heading for Rotterdam.

Of course, Jasper Broxton knows nothing of this. For him, the only thought at the forefront of his mind is to try to discover where Ackroyd & Guskett have relocated. He presumes there must have been some problem with the tenancy. It has happened to him in his career. A landlord requires the premises for another use. A letter asking the occupant to leave is dispatched, though he admits to being slightly unnerved by the comment about unpaid rent. But he reassures himself that there is bound to be a reason. There is always a reason.

Broxton finds the nearest cab rank and orders the cabby to take him to his club. This is where he first met

Anton Guskett, and where he is quite sure he will either find him, news of him, or an address where he can be located. There will be an explanation. Trust is at the heart of any business transaction, he tells himself, conveniently forgetting the number of people who trusted him in the past with their savings and have been grievously let down as a consequence.

After a short journey, he alights at the door of his club. He hands in his coat, hat and stick to the doorman, then makes a quick tour of the various rooms to see if Anton Guskett is there. Not finding him, he sidles up to Leary, the head waiter, and inquires, as casually as he can, if Mr Guskett has dined here recently. Leary frowns, shakes his head, and says no, come to think of it, sir, he has not seen the gentleman for a couple of weeks, which in his opinion is unusual as he enjoys his club dinners and his conversations with other members. He hopes as how Mr Guskett has not met with an accident, or, heaven forfend, gone down with this here plague that is supposed to be rampaging all over London, although he, Leary has to admit he is beginning to think it is all some sort of hoax to sell newspapers as he has not seen any dead bodies.

Seriously alarmed by this revelation, Broxton now applies to the club secretary for the address of Anton Guskett, explaining that it is a matter of urgent business. After some harumphing and muttering that it is not the usual procedure to give out the private details of club members, and the proffering of certain inducements to persuade him to do so, Broxton is furnished with the address. Leaving the club, he makes his way straight to the block of apartments where Anton Guskett has a set of bachelor rooms. There, he is informed that Mr Guskett has left the building, taking all his belongings with him. And owing three weeks' rent and the salary of the manservant he hired to look after his needs.

And now, finally, the situation becomes crystal clear to him. He has been duped by these two men. The friendly overtures made by the flashy and affable Guskett, the brandies bought, cigars proffered, the dinners provided, were all a lure to get him to part with his money, which they have stolen from him. He has been traduced! He has been swindled! He has been robbed!

Broxton feels the anger rising up in him, followed swiftly by a burning desire to exact revenge. He will report the men to the police ~ yes, he will go straight round to Scotland Yard and let the forces of law-and-order deal with them. And when they are captured and brought to trial, he will testify in a court of law as to their bad character and watch as they are taken down to spend the rest of their miserable lives in Pentonville prison. Or the colonies. His fury giving his feet wings, Jasper Broxton sets out upon his mission.

*****

Detective Sergeant Jack Cully has had a quiet week. There is nothing like the threat of a deadly disease to keep the usual suspects off the streets and confined to their own houses. Crime has gone down. Lunacy has gone up, but that is not necessarily a criminal matter. It is therefore a relief when he is summoned to the front desk by a constable who tells him a man has just arrived to report the robbery of a considerable sum of money.

Cully migrates to the entrance lobby where he finds a well-dressed man sitting on the edge of the Anxious Bench, his face red, his expression furious. At the sight of Cully, he springs to his feet and hurries towards him.

"Are you one of the detectives?" he demands hotly. "I have been robbed. Swindled. The men I put my trust in have repaid it by emptying my bank account!" This is not strictly true ~ as the money came mainly from other people's bank accounts, but Broxton has a fine line in mendacious and inflammatory rhetoric. And ethics.

Jack Cully waits until the tirade has come to an end, then says calmly: "If you'd care to follow me, sir, I'll take down the particulars of the events. Then we can discuss a possible way forward."

Broxton's eyes open wide, and his hands bunch into white-knuckled fists. If he were a horse, he'd be foaming at the mouth and striking out with his front hooves. "A *possible* way forward? What nonsense is this? There is only one way forward! The thieves must be caught at once and subjected to the full force of the law!"

Ah, Cully thinks, we have one of those. The sort who thinks the world moves at their command. He is glad Stride is currently occupied somewhere in the basement: his dislike for this type of individual is legendary and sometimes unhelpful, as he tended, in the past, to display it to their faces. Leading the way to his small office, Cully indicates that his visitor may sit, which he does, with the air of a sulky schoolboy summoned to see the headmaster.

"Now, please may I have your name, your address, and an outline of the incident you wish me to investigate," Cully says calmly.

Broxton complies with the request, then relates the course of his unfortunate relationship with Edward Ackroyd and Anton Guskett. He is so absorbed in enunciating the various deceptions and tricks as he perceives them, and his sense of grievance as a result, that he fails to notice that Cully has set down his pen and is regarding him steadily. Eventually, it dawns on him that no notes are being taken on the other side of the desk. Broxton folds his arms and glares.

"You seem rather uninterested in my predicament, officer," he says peevishly. "I assure you, to lose such a great sum of money is no indifferent matter to me."

"Oh, I share your concern, believe me," Cully replies. "And as I have all the relevant details, I shall commence my enquiries on your behalf at once. We will correspond with you as soon as we have any information." He rises, signalling that the meeting is over.

Huffing slightly, Broxton leaves Scotland Yard. He would have liked a little bit more sympathy from the police detective. However, his dilemma now is how to keep his creditors off his back long enough to build up his reserves once more. He returns to his office and prepares another tranche of advertisements. The prospective investors won't know that Ackroyd and Guskett and their lucrative government contract no longer exist, so if he front-loads his portfolio with new capital, he can once again pay off Peter using Paul's money, as it were. At least until he inherits the Broxton lands and fortune, which, given the predicament he currently finds himself in, cannot come soon enough.

Meanwhile Jack Cully seeks out the head of the Detective Division, whom he finds instructing one of the newest recruits in the art of preparing a police report for a coroner's inquiry. Greig takes one look at Cully's face and quietly tells the young detective they will resume later. After the door closes, Cully shares what he has just been told by Jasper Broxton. Greig listens intently, then gives a brief nod of understanding.

"First, we need to telegraph the Whitechapel Police Office and see if they can shed any light on this matter," he says. "Once we hear back, we'll make a decision as to how to proceed."

Cully goes to arrange for the telegraph to be sent. The answer comes back within the hour: the man named Mr Anton Guskett reported in once. They have not seen anything of the second man, and the assumption was subsequently made that both must have chosen to report to Greig, as he was the one issuing the orders. Greig and Cully have a quick meeting and decide to send a constable along to the construction site to see whether the men are still there.

The report comes back that the site is closed, and according to neighbours, has been quiet for some time. Greig takes the decision to issue an all-police offices alert. After all, they are now not only dealing with two irresponsible individuals who have disobeyed his orders, they have just been alerted to further criminal activity. Not that they hold out much hope of catching the men after the time that has now elapsed. Too much water has flowed under the bridge, as Cully observes trenchantly. It is a prescient comment, although he doesn't know it yet.

****

The Thames Division of the Metropolitan Police is headquartered at Wapping, a little above the entrance of the old Thames tunnel. It looks out over the river, just at the junction of the Lower and Upper Pool. It is currently under the control of Superintendent Micah Wilks, who has under him thirty-one inspectors, three sergeants and one hundred and fifteen constables.

Every night, rain or fine, four to six boats can be generally found rowing guard in different parts of the river, manned by constables in their distinctive uniform of blue double-breasted jackets and hard glazed hats.

Apart from catching smugglers, an important part of their duties consists in searching for and dealing with the bodies of suicides, murdered persons and the accidentally drowned. Generally, they only check for one tide, after which it is generally thought that a corpse will have been carried out of reach. Occasionally though, a body will drift into a hole and won't rise to the surface until it becomes sufficiently buoyant. The U-bend of the Thames around the Isle of Dogs is a trapping point for bodies that tend to accumulate from all sections of the river.

Thus, on a clear night, with a sky full of stars and the tide running high, the night-guard of K division, which holds the bank of the river at Stepney, is on duty. Their oars dip and rattle in the rowlocks, the light on the boat's stern flickering in the inky blackness. The barges and hulks form a black wall on either side, their chains rattling and clanking. Here and there, a coal fire in an iron cresset blazes on a nearby wharf. Uncomfortable rushings of water suggestive of gurgling and drowning accompanies the plash of their oars The men row on until suddenly, the boat bumps against a body floating in the water. They pull it on board with their long hooked poles and bring it to land, where in the morning it will be photographed and examined for signs of violence, before being placed at the parish dead-house to await identification.

A 'Body Found' bill is duly posted, and a message sent round other London police offices to that effect, in the hope that someone might have reported a missing person. The message is placed upon the desk of Jack Cully, eventually working its way to the top of a pile of similar messages, where something about the contents sets alarm bells ringing and is the reason that Cully is even now hurrying across London to Wapping, where after initial inquiries, he is shown into a small whitewashed room, similar to that occupied by Robertson, where the body is being kept prior to burial.

After briefly viewing and identifying the corpse, Cully is shown the autopsy report, which indicates the amount of arsenic discovered in the stomach of the deceased. He is also shown a gold ring and a gold watch and chain, both found on the deceased, which bear the initials E.A. confirming that this is indeed the body of Edward Ackroyd. On his return, Cully seeks a meeting with Lachlan Greig, to whom he reports his sad discovery. "Given the circumstances of his unfortunate demise, I wonder whether Mr Ackroyd met his unfortunate end at the hands of his partner," he muses, after handing Greig a copy of the autopsy report.

Greig nods thoughtfully. "I confess that my thoughts are travelling in the self-same direction, Jack. The use of poison, coupled with the disappearance of Anton Guskett, and combined with the closure of their joint bank account, is highly suspicious. I recall the man Guskett at our interview ~ he was too confident by half. Clearly, he had already made plans. So now it appears that we have a murder inquiry on our hands, as well as a case of fraud. I will write to Mr Broxton, not that the information will be of any consolation to him at all, as I doubt our man will still be in London."

"Should we alert the port authorities?" Cully asks.

"Always worth sending round a description," Greig agrees. "Though I expect, if he has any sense, he will already be abroad somewhere, counting his ill-gotten gains. I very much fear that Mr Jasper Broxton will never see him or his money again."

****

It has now been several weeks since the orphan Ruth moved from her communal dormitory to the London house of Clara and Margaret Broxton to begin her new life as the future Broxton heiress. With the city struck down by (imaginary) plague, the newly minted Miss Ruth Broxton has been confined to quarters, where she has spent her time getting to know her mother ~ a woman with whom she has had no relationship whatsoever for the whole of her life. All of the young orphan girl's childhood has passed within the stark, regimented walls of a charity orphanage, so that it would be a miracle indeed if her sudden transportation to a well-furnished private house with new-found relations and servants at her beck and call, could be accomplished smoothly and without problems.

And alas, there have been problems.

Here are the newly-formed family at the breakfast table. The redoubtable Miss Broxton, or 'Aunt' as she has told Ruth to call her, is once again keeping a close watch on the girl's behaviour. "Now, Ruth dear, I believe you have been told not to reach across the table like that," she says. "If you want anything, either indicate to the maid, or ask me or your Mama."

The girl Ruth pulls a face. "Can I have a bit of toast?"

"May I have a slice of toast, please and yes, you may. Sarah ~ Miss Ruth would like some toast."

The maid steps forward, picks up the silver toast rack and offers it to the girl.

"Always take the outside piece," her aunt advises. "And then only one pat of butter, and a small spoonful of preserve on the side of your plate. Sarah, please place Miss Ruth's napkin upon her lap, she seems to have forgotten it again."

Margaret Broxton, new mother, and long-term invalid, smiles weakly and sips her cup of tea. She has been persuaded to rouse herself from her former torpor to help train up her daughter for the role she will be expected to assume in the future. It is proving to be much harder than she thought.

Margaret imagined the girl would just slip into their London life as if she had always been part of it. She envisioned long afternoons lying on the chaise-longue with Ruth reading to her from the Ladies' Magazine, or one of Mrs Henry Wood's novels. It had been a shock to discover that her daughter's literary ability, although competent, was certainly not up to reading a novel. And then there was the question of her voice. Ruth's pronunciation and enunciation are more fitting for below than above stairs. Already, her sister is talking of engaging an elocution tutor. And the girl clatters everywhere in her boots, when all the servants wear slippers to preserve the silence Margaret Broxton requests as a suffering woman, and once, she is sure she'd heard Ruth singing an unsuitable song.

But the most troubling aspect of the new arrival is her own lack of maternal feelings. Try as she might, she simply can not summon up the necessary emotions. Margaret puts it down to the unfortunate circumstances surrounding her daughter's conception and birth, closely followed by her disappearance into an orphanage. Even so, and despite the past, she is sure that she *ought* to feel something, but as she studies her daughter's face which is rather plain, with glassy blue eyes, a snub nose and fair hair that has been washed, then brushed the requisite fifty times each morning and evening, but still straggles limply to her shoulders, she finds to her chagrin that she experiences no warm gush of maternal love for the child whatsoever. It is like being in the presence of a complete stranger. She tries to get round it by calling her 'my child' or 'dear Ruthie' but she is pretty sure the girl isn't fooled. She certainly isn't. But for the moment, Margaret is happy to let her daughter's education devolve to her sister, who now rises from her seat in a purposeful manner.

"Have you finished your breakfast, Ruth? If so, I suggest you return to your room and prepare yourself for the day ahead. As the threat of plague seems to have abated from our streets, it is my intention that we shall visit Tussaud's Wax Exhibition this morning. We will regard the magnificent figures representing the Queen's Coronation and view the Royal Family at Home tableaux."

Ruth sets down her knife with an air of weariness. "When can I see my friends again?" she inquires, staring down at her plate.

The sisters exchange a horrified glance over the top of her bent head.

"But Ruthie dear," Margaret says patiently, "do you not understand? You are no longer an orphan. You have a mama and a kind aunt. Surely you do not want to remind yourself of that place where you were alone and without the joy of a family of your own?"

The girl gives her a dark side-glance from under her eyelids. Then, compressing her lips firmly, she gets up from her place and walks out of the room, kicking the leg of a chair as she goes. A few seconds later, her boots can be heard thumping noisily up the stairs. Margaret winces and passes a limp wrist across her alabaster brow.

"I really don't want to make a fuss Clara, but are we sure Ruth is my daughter? Really sure? After all, we have never seen the shawl she was wrapped in, nor my locket ..." her voice tails off into uncomfortable silence. She shifts in her chair, clasping her mittened hands together compulsively.

Miss Broxton regards her sister severely. "But we both met the woman in charge of the orphanage, if you recall. She explained how many tokens just got lost in the move. We decided from the evidence of the official records that the girl was the most likely child to have been your baby. Yes, I admit I am disappointed with her too, but we must recall she has not been out of that place for her whole life. She is like some native savage, and it is our job to instil into her uneducated soul our civilized attitudes and Christian behaviour.

"Remember what Doctor Swinson said about your health, sister? Any moment, your heart could give out. Do you want our dear parents' money and property to pass to our cousin Jasper and his deplorable wife? Do you want your own sister to be turned out into the street?"

Margaret bites her lower lip. "No, of course not," she quavers.

"Then let us not have this conversation again. I will use the visit to Tussauds to instruct Ruth in the correct behaviour required at the breakfast table. It may take time, but we will make a Broxton out of her. Now, I shall go and prepare for the day and Sarah can clear the breakfast table. I suggest you return to your room and rest."

The sisters leave the room arm in arm, the one leaning, the other supporting. Meanwhile Sarah ~ aka Avice Broxton's spy, begins to pile crockery onto a tray, her mind busily running over the conversation she has just heard. She decides that as soon as she has taken the tray down to the scullery, she will write a letter to her mistress asking for an urgent meeting. The information might be worth quite a bit of money. How lucky that the gentry never notice those who stand and wait! And in this case, how very unfortunate for them.

****

Later that afternoon, wearing her best bonnet (because it is her afternoon off) Sarah the spy enters a quiet tearoom ~ the sort frequented by married ladies with a generous allowance who spend their time shopping. There, she waits patiently at a window table until Avice Broxton enters and joins her. Late. As usual.

"I have read your letter," Avice says, without greeting her. She removes her expensive grey gloves and places them, and her expensive matching bag, on the adjoining seat. "We are most interested by your news."

The spy glances at the next table, where two well-dressed women are tucking into scones and cakes. They look delicious. She transfers her glance back to Avice, clearing her throat in a thirsty manner.

"Do you require tea?" Avice says. "I have had some before I came out. Let us discuss your news first, shall we? Now, I want to hear more about this locket. You say the girl does not possess it?"

Sarah nods. "I distinctly heard Miss Margaret say it."

"Of course, it could have been lost," Avice muses. "Such things happen. Or perhaps it was stolen. A valuable piece of jewellery ..."

"But there was a shawl too," Sarah persists. "Nobody would take a shawl, would they? It ain't of any value. And there's something else: I seen a pitcher of Miss Margaret when she was young, and she had long dark hair and dark eyes. The girl looks nothing like her."

"I see. Nothing like her at all," Avice fiddles with her hat pin. "How *very* interesting."

There is a pause. Then,

"Now, look here, Missis," Sarah says boldly. "I done everything you arsked me. Now I want to leave this job. I ain't happy working there. It really doesn't suit me anymore. I thought, maybe, you could employ me instead. I'm a good worker, reliable. You can trust me. As you know."

Avice's pale eyes open wide in astonishment. "Oh, I don't think that would be possible, Sarah," she says, evenly. "No, not possible at all. I have a full staff already and due to various unfortunate events, we are currently having to retrench considerably. Besides, I am relying on you to supply me with further information about my husband's cousins and this girl they are clearly trying to pass off as a member of their family. I should be most put out if you left their employ. Most put out indeed."

Sarah pinches her lips together. "Like I said, Missis, I find I'm not suited. Of course, if it was made worth my while to stay, that might go some way to changing my mind. If you catch my drift."

Avice gives her a hard stare. "You have been amply rewarded, in my opinion, Sarah," she says sharply. "I am not made of money. As I said, we are having to make cutbacks to our own lives. I cannot stop you leaving your job, but if you choose to do so, I may have to write to my husband's cousins and inform them that you have been secretly supplying me with information. Of course, I would write anonymously. But you may discover if you leave with no testimonial, it would make it hard to find future employment. I'm sure you understand what I am saying? Now, here is some money for your last letter. If you learn anything else, I shall always be glad to receive your information." And with this, Avice rises, picks up her bag and gloves, and walks out of the tea-room.

Sarah the spy pockets the coins, her face darkening. So the mean cow isn't prepared to help her? Not even to a cup of tea? Very well. So be it. She has been mulling over an idea for the past few weeks, ever since the girl arrived. Maybe it is now time to put her idea into action.

****

Summer has turned its back on London, and with its departure, has taken the threat of plague from the streets. As the daytime weather cools, the fear of imminent disease and death recedes. Felix Lawrence, general surgeon, makes his way to the London Hospital, observing with relief that the man in the black coat and high cravat, who spent much of the day sitting in an open carriage outside the main entrance, urging his fellow Londoners not to cross the threshold, as the hospital was full of infected plague victims, has taken himself and his bizarre protest elsewhere. There is only so long one can maintain a daytime vigil in the face of no visible evidence whatsoever.

The city is gradually coming back to itself. The ghosts have departed the streets. The affluent have returned to their mansions. Nothing strange has been fished out of the Thames nor discovered lurking in the sewers for some time. Even the street cats are no longer skulking furtively along the far edges of the footways but seem to have regained their former bold swagger.

Here are Jack Cully and Violet, on their morning walk to the omnibus stop. School has resumed after the break, and Violet is wearing a new tunic and smart coat, the finishing touches having been put in last night by her devoted mother, for both his daughters spent the 'plague' summer with their grandparents in the countryside, revelling in the tiny attic bedroom in the pretty cottage that dated back to medieval times and is like a dolls' house. Every day they explored the town, visited the local market, breathed good country air, and stuffed themselves on fresh eggs, bread, butter and other good things. As a result, both girls have sprouted up like weeds and Cully has had to dig deep to find money for clothes, shoes, and boots.

Violet leads the way, her new satchel bouncing on her back. Cully is happy to listen to her chatter, while he mentally reviews the case reports beginning to pile up on his desk once again. It is as if, to make up for their absence from the streets, the criminal fraternity have redoubled their efforts after the plague scare has evaporated. Nevertheless, despite the increase in crime, he is happy to see the city back to its normal self ~ even though a few cautious citizens are still sporting cotton or silk face coverings and avoiding walking too close to other passers-by.

Ex-Detective Inspector Leo Stride rejoices to see that the coffee-stall holders have returned to their former position on the corner of the piazza, looking none the worse for their absence. Indeed, as the old man tells him, while his wife is preparing a mug of the noxious black brew Stride likes to drink, they spent the time visiting a relative of the wife's in Bournemouth, "and very pleasant it was to escape the grim and grime of London, no offence, Mr Stride and that'll be tuppence sir, if you please."

Stride receives his drink, pays for it and continues on his way. No wild-eyed, bearded men approach him with inky pamphlets proclaiming, 'The End of the Wrold'. The people crossing the piazza look like normal everyday individuals pursuing their daily round and allotted tasks. Smiling to himself, Stride enters the building that has been his place of work for so many years and is now a place of sanctuary from the ongoing demands of Mrs Stride. Greeting the desk constable, he carries his coffee carefully down to the basement, where the latest box file of case reports awaits his scrutiny. He has a new notebook, and a new title: *A*

Constable on the Cobbles. Time to recommence his memoirs.

Meanwhile young Violet Cully steps off the omnibus and walks the short distance to the school building, where she positions herself by the railings as she waits for her friend May to arrive. The girls have not seen each other during the holidays, and Violet has much to tell her. Eventually, she sees a hansom approaching the gate, but this is not the smart shiny cab with Prince pulling it, his mane and tail be-ribboned. This is a decrepit old vehicle, pulled by a dusty looking horse. And the driver isn't May's father, but an elderly man in a battered top hat. The cab stops at the kerb. The door opens, and May tumbles out. The two girls embrace. Then May waves goodbye, and with a limp flourish of his whip, the cabby drives off.

"Where is your pa today; is he unwell?" Violet asks anxiously.

"Oh Vi," May pulls a face, "Pa's cab was in an accident last week, and it is broken beyond repair. It wasn't his fault: a carrier's cart came round the corner far too fast and ran straight into the side of him."

"And Prince?"

May bites her lip, "He fell over and hurt himself. We had to ... to ..." her eyes fill with tears.

Violet stands next to her friend, helplessly patting her shoulder. "I am so so sorry, May," she says. "He was a lovely horse."

"He was the very best horse in the world," May sighs. "But now Pa has to find the money for another cab, and another horse. It is very hard on us. That's why he didn't drive me to school. He has gone looking for a job. Luckily everybody in the cab trade knows and respects him ~ so somebody else is going to bring me to school until we get back on our feet."

Arm in arm, the two girls make their way into the school building and head for the cloakroom, where they hang up their coats on adjacent pegs. Turning round, they spy Johanna Broxton staring at them with undisguised scorn. Violet folds her arms and glares back at her.

"Oh, I am *so* terrified," Johanna smirks. She gives both girls a slow insolent once-over. "Dear, dear," she says, "look at your tunic, May Higgs. I can see exactly where it has been let down. How undignified. And your coat is missing a button. How can your parents let you come to a good school like this looking like a rag-picker's child? And what on earth was that broken down old contraption you arrived in? Shameful."

"No, it is *you* who are shameful!" Violet says hotly, taking a couple of steps forward. "There are more important things in this world than carriages and new clothes. But I don't expect you'd understand, so I will not waste my breath explaining it to you. Come May, we are missing valuable lesson time," and grabbing her friend by the arm, she steers her away.

"My father is a rich businessman, and we live in one of the best addresses in London, Violet Cully," Johanna calls after them. "Your father is only a common policeman."

Violet spins round, daggers in her eyes. "My father," she says, icicles hanging from every word, "is a top police detective at Scotland Yard. So you'd better watch out, Johanna Broxton, 'coz one day, he may well be coming for you."

"You are so brave," May murmurs as the two enter their classroom. "I am not sure I have the courage to stand up to her like you do."

"I just imagine in my mind that I am bold Horatius," Violet replies, squeezing her friend's arm, "and of course, Johanna Broxton is false Sextus. And we both know how that encounter ended."

****

Chief Inspector Lachlan Greig does not usually take any notice of the newsboys who stand at the corners of streets, shouting the headlines as they sell their daily papers. Partly because he knows a selection of the morning papers will have already been placed upon his desk awaiting his attention, and partly because he is usually deep in his own thoughts as he walks to Scotland Yard. Today however, his attention is caught by a small boy in a large cloth cap bawling at the top of his voice: "*Broxton Heiress Is A Fake ~ Foul Play Suspected! Read all about it!*"

It is the word 'Broxton' that catches him unawares. He had a meeting with a Mr Jasper Broxton recently. Same man? A possibility. Greig quickens his pace. It looks as if an investigation he thought had run into the sand has unexpectedly resurrected itself. He enters his office and riffles through the pile of newspapers left for him. As he suspected, given the sensational headline, it is *The Inquirer* that carries the story on its front page. Two lines down elicits the information that this is not the Broxton individual he has had dealings with. This story is about the discovery of a young girl, who is supposed to be the lost daughter of one of two wealthy sisters. But further reading proves instructive. The piece suggests that she is a ringer, brought in to secure the future inheritance of said rich sisters. It ends with a quote from a Mr Jasper Broxton, entrepreneur, affirming that "*There is no proof that the girl is or ever was a relative. In my opinion, it is evidence of the desperation of my cousins to deny members of my family their rightful claim to the Broxton inheritance.*"

Greig tosses the paper aside. Stories of lost heirs turning up unexpectedly to claim their inheritance are two-a-penny. Ditto lost heirs subsequently vanishing without trace, usually carrying said inheritance in some portable form. However, this is clearly a family matter, not a police matter and subsequently of little concern to him. He has written to Mr Jasper Broxton about the discovery of the drowned body, and suggested that, pending further information, the Detective Division is unable to proceed further in recovering his stolen money.

But the story is of great interest elsewhere in the capital. Miss Lucy Landseer also heard a news boy shouting the headlines on her way to her Consulting Room at 122A Baker Street and reluctantly, because she too has a pretty low opinion of the paper and its chief reporter, purchased a copy of *The Inquirer*, which she is currently reading while sitting at her desk.

The outcome is unfortunate but comes as no real surprise. In a previous incarnation, Lucy Landseer, under an ambiguously gendered *nom-de-plume* penned a thrilling series of crime novels featuring daring lady detective Belle Batchelor and her faithful canine side-kick, Harris. Now, she clothes herself (mentally) in the bonnet of her alter-ego and runs through a few likely scenarios.

Who benefits financially ~ that is always the baseline question, she thinks. In this case, it is Mr Jasper Broxton, who stands to inherit everything if no female child exists. His motives are clear: disprove the validity of the girl's provenance. But then her mind turns to Miss Broxton and her sister. They are also beneficiaries. Were they too hasty in their choice? After all, they had no real proof that the orphan they selected really was Margaret's child. Did their desire to thwart their cousin override basic common sense?

How right the great playwright William Shakespeare was when he wrote about complicated webs of deception. Or words to that effect. Here were three spiders, all spinning away busily. It would make a wonderful plot for a story. Her reverie is broken by the sound of rapid footsteps mounting the stairs followed by a series of rapid knocks at her door. Lucy rises and approaches the door. With sudden prescience, she knows exactly who is standing on the other side.

****

Stride has spent a productive morning working through a number of back cases. He has made copious notes, drunk several mugs of noxious coffee (there is always a young constable sufficiently in awe of his past reputation to be inveigled into fetching his beverage from the coffee stall holders). Now it is midday, and he is on his way to enjoy his usual hot luncheon (chop, baked potato, glass of ale and a chat) at his favourite watering hole, recently reopened for business.

Passing through the front office, he is surprised to hear his name being called in a firm, bright voice from someone seated on the Anxious Bench. Turning, Stride sees a handsome young woman with inquisitive blue eyes and hair the colour of untamed treacle. Sitting next to her is a stout, dour-faced older woman dressed in a plain but well-made tailored suit and a severe bonnet.

Stride pauses. The young woman hurries over.

"Good day Detective Inspector Stride," she says. "You do not remember me, of course. I am Miss Lucy Landseer. We met some years ago. The Metropolitan Madonna? I helped you to solve that strange case. And," she adds, her eyes twinkling roguishly, "at the time, you complimented me. You called me a 'very clever young woman', as I recall."

"Did I indeed?"

"You did. As you see from my card, I am now in the same line of work as yourself. And I'd like to call in the favour I did for you and Detective Cully: I have a former client who requires your help."

Lucy indicates the woman seated on the bench. "Her name is Miss Clara Broxton. I see the name does not provoke any reaction. Her story, or a version of it, is currently gracing the front page of *The Inquirer* ~ yes, Mr Richard Dandy's handiwork once again. Please will you speak to her? I am in the throes of several new inquiries and am unable to offer her the expert assistance she urgently seeks."

Stride is just about to inform the young woman that sadly, he has retired from the Detective Division and so cannot be of any help, when the door to the outside world opens, admitting Jack Cully. His eyes light up at the sight of the pair.

"Why, it's Miss ... Landseer!" he exclaims. "It has been some time since we last met. How do you do?"

"Well enough, detective," Lucy dimples. "And what a good memory you have! I was just telling your esteemed colleague: I have started my own private detective agency now."

"My eldest daughter will be thrilled when I tell her," Cully smiles. "She often says she intends to become a detective when she grows up."

"I hope she does, then," Lucy nods. "For it is a fascinating profession. And one that needs the feminine perspective on so many occasions. And it is in my professional capacity that I am here today. A former client needs help. It is a complicated matter, and one that requires delicacy and discretion. Alas, I am unable to deal with it. And I think, having heard her story, that it is a police matter." She opens her bag. "I have made some notes from my previous meetings with Miss Broxton. I suggest Detective Inspector Stride might like to read through them before speaking to her. It will set the scene and provide him with some important background information."

And with that, Lucy returns to the Anxious Bench, where she conducts a hurried conversation with the older woman, before cordially bidding her farewell. Stride and Cully look from each other to the bench. The woman gives them a hopeful smile.

"There will be a copy of *The Inquirer* on Lachlan's desk," Cully says. "I will ask one of the constables to fetch it. I wonder if the lady is any relation to the Mr Jasper Broxton we had dealings with recently ~ a case of financial fraud and deception. Interesting. I shall go and introduce myself to her."

Stride opens his mouth to remind Cully that he is retired. Then closes it again. After all, it was him that Miss Landseer appealed to first. He is the one she recommended. He decides to tag along quietly in the background. On a purely observational basis.

****

If Miss Clara Broxton and her ailing sister Margaret had assumed all their troubles were over with the discovery of the child they abandoned at birth, they were soon to be disabused. The sorry tale that Miss Broxton related to the two detectives showed that while you can take a girl from an orphanage, the reverse does not necessarily apply.

Ruth had absolutely no preparation for her new life. She was suddenly thrust from a communal existence, with all its petty rules and regulations, into a totally different world. Initially, she reacted so well ~

revelling in her new clothes, her own room with its pretty writing desk and canopied bed. She gobbled down the well-cooked meals and appeared humbled and grateful to the two sisters who were now her parent and guardian.

But, it did not last. After the initial 'honeymoon' period, Ruth began to assert herself. What the sisters had judged to be her sweet gentle nature now showed itself in small obstinate refusals to obey. She complained about having to study. She did not want to accompany Clara on her afternoon walks, preferring to loll around in her room. Worst of all, she began to exhibit a marked prejudice against Margaret, her mama, taking every opportunity when they were alone, to bombard her with questions about why she had been abandoned.

"My sister was getting to the end of her resources with the girl," Miss Broxton told the detectives. "Her health, which was always precarious, began to go downhill at an alarming rate. She started spending more and more time confined to bed, and Ruth absolutely refused point blank to sit with her. The obstinacy of the girl was quite unbelievable, given that she was her own dear child."

The situation was not helped by a series of letters from Cousin Jasper and from his solicitor, demanding documentary proof that Ruth actually was the real daughter of his cousin Margaret and inferring that court papers were being prepared and she might have to supply such proofs to a judge.

But events were about to take a dramatic and unexpected turn. Four days ago, Ruth had been preparing to visit the Zoological Gardens in the company of her aunt. Her mother was expecting a visit from the doctor. While the doctor was in attendance, accompanied by Miss Broxton as chaperone, the girl must have slipped out of the front door.

It was assumed at first that she had gone for a walk on her own. However, as the hours passed and she did not return, the sisters began to feel uneasy, and when night fell and she still had not returned, panic set in. Every inch of the house was searched, in case she was hiding. Attic, kitchen, every wardrobe, and cupboard were examined. Next morning at first light, the servants scoured the streets, calling her name. Local shops were visited to see if she had called in to purchase anything. A letter was written and dispatched to the orphanage, seeking to know if she had turned up. The reply came back that she had not been seen since the day she left.

"I cannot believe that Ruth would deliberately run off, given the wonderful new life she had been offered. I can only therefore assume that she quit the house to evade our excursion and was subsequently seized by somebody who knew that she was due to inherit the Broxton fortune. My finger of suspicion points directly to our cousin Jasper, who, if he was not directly involved, may well have instructed some low ruffian to take the girl. I would not put anything past him and his vile wife.

"I also do not know who gave the story to the newspaper," Miss Broxton continued. "I have my suspicions though and they point the same way. One of our maidservants disappeared very shortly after the girl vanished, and I now gather from our cook that she was spotted writing letters to Avice Broxton and occasionally seen leaving the house to meet up with her. Clearly she was also working for Avice Broxton. I suggest that you begin your investigations there."

After Miss Broxton finally leaves Scotland Yard, Cully and Stride compare impressions.

"I am always amazed that people of a certain class think that the normal rules do not apply to them," Stride muses. "The girl has been missing for four days. And yet this lady waits until now to contact us. And we weren't even her first port of call."

Cully purses his lips. "I should like to interview Mrs Avice Broxton, though. Those letters from the maidservant may throw some light on events. Especially as to who has talked to the press. But first, I shall let Greig know about this meeting. We have had recent dealings with Mr Jasper Broxton over a business matter. It may be unconnected, but even so, I'm sure Greig will want to be brought into this investigation."

Cully pulls a sheet of paper towards him and begins writing the notes he will share later with his colleague.

Stride notes the 'I'. Once again, he is being politely reminded that he is no longer part of the establishment. He has no authority here. He rises and mutters something about lunch and returning to his memoirs. But as he makes his way out, a thought occurs: Jack Cully mentioned nothing about questioning the remaining Broxton servants. So, were he, Stride, to casually find himself outside the house, which could easily happen, it might be interesting to see what they have to say. He may have no part in the official investigation, but Miss Landseer's briefing notes were addressed to him. And he seems to have picked them up on his way out.

After a hearty lunch at Sally's Chop House, Stride decides to take the afternoon off. It is a fine day, and he decides that a postprandial walk is in order. He sets out and arrives shortly at the street where Miss Broxton and her sister are living. Stride strolls down one side of the footway, glancing at the house numbers until he arrives opposite the property, where he realises there are no steps down to the kitchen area, so he can only access the domestic staff by ringing the front doorbell.

Stride walks on a little further, mulling over his options. When he turns round, he sees that the front door of the house has opened, and a maid is standing on the step glancing up the road in the opposite direction. Her expression is anxious, and she is wringing her hands compulsively. A few seconds later, she is joined by another maid. The two servants conduct a hurried conversation. One then ventures out into the road, sees Stride approaching, and hurries across to him.

"Oh sir, here you are at last!" she cries, clutching the sleeve of his coat. "You must hurry, sir. We don't know what to do for the best." Next minute, much to his surprise, Stride finds himself being dragged across the street and into the house, where, lying at the bottom of the stairs, he sees the crumpled form of a woman clad in her nightclothes. From the position of her body, and the twisted angle of her neck, it is quite clear that she is dead.

Stride's hand automatically strays into his pocket, where it finds the ever-present notebook. From his first day in the force until now, he has never been without a notebook and an accompanying pencil. It has been a long time since he has personally found a dead person, but he begins to go through the never-forgotten rituals, noting down the relation of the body to its surroundings, the position of the body, and the place and surface upon which it is lying. Finally, he writes a description of the woman's clothing.

While he writes, the house servants stand in the hallway, mute and watchful. Having finished his preliminary investigation, Stride closes the notebook. He glances round.

"Can someone identify for me who this is?" he says.

"It's the mistress, Miss Margaret, poor lady."

"And are you able to say how she ended up at the bottom of the stairs?"

"I can tell you that, sir," one of the maids says, her voice bordering upon tears. "I was with her in her room when we heard the sound of wheels outside in the street. Straightway Miss Margaret sat up in bed and said, 'Oh, it is Ruth! I am sure it is her! She has returned to us. I must go down and greet her.' Then she got up and ran out onto the landing. Only you see sir, she was very weak ~ the shock of Miss Ruth, who is her long-lost daughter, going so suddenly like she did, had brought on her old troubles. And before I could stop her, she had tripped on the top step and fallen down to the bottom. I ran down after her, calling her name, but she didn't move."

"Has a doctor been sent for?"

"Yes. But … you aren't the doctor?"

Stride rapidly joins up a few ends. So that explains the anxious housemaids on the steps, and the reason why he has been dragged unceremoniously into the house. He is on the cusp of explaining his presence when the front door opens and a frock-coated man carrying a leather bag hurries into the hallway. He is out of breath.

Stride steps away from the body. "Doctor? Leo Stride, Scotland Yard." (Well, it is true as far as it goes). "I'm afraid there is little you can do here. The lady has suffered a catastrophic fall." He motions the servants to stand aside, as the doctor approaches the body of Margaret Broxton, kneels down and places two fingers gently against the twisted neck. He looks up and nods. "There is no pulse." He gets to his feet. "Alas, I was attending another patient, or I would have arrived sooner ~ maybe in time to save her."

Stride doubts this very much. A fall from that height, even for a strong man, would result in broken bones, maybe a severe head injury. From what he has read, Miss Margaret Broxton was frail, unhealthy, and delicate. Sadly, the outcome was never in doubt.

"But you say you are from Scotland Yard?" the doctor queries. "Do you bring news of the little girl? Has she been found?"

Stride shakes his head.

"Ah. I understand," the doctor says. "Such a tragedy. My patient was distraught when she disappeared. Her heart ~ you know, it was always weak. I am sure she would have appreciated the courtesy of your visit, even though you brought her no good news. Well, well, too late now." He opens his medical bag. "If you would excuse me, officer. I must make an examination of the body and prepare my report for the coroner, before the servants begin to lay her out. Poor lady, she and her sister were so happy when the girl was discovered. I suppose her sister doesn't yet know what has occurred?"

Stride shakes his head.

"It will be a blow. Yes indeed. A great blow. They were very close, you know. Miss Broxton has been devoted to her sister for as long as I have known them." He moves away from Stride, shaking his head sadly. The conversation is over.

Stride collects his hat from the hall stand, takes a final look around, and shows himself out. The servants are too busy clustering round the doctor to notice his departure.

****

Meanwhile, unaware of the tragedy unfolding at her home, Miss Clara Broxton has decided to seize time by the forelock. She sets a course straight from Scotland Yard to Regent's Park, where here she is, beating in an alarming fashion on the black-painted door of the mid-terrace property that houses her cousin and his wife. After a few seconds, showing no restraint whatsoever and careless of the curious glances of passersby, she starts shouting, "Open this door! Open it at once, I say!"

Eventually, a scared-looking maid responds to her cries. Miss Broxton thrusts her aside and storms into the hallway. "Where is she?" she demands.

The maid tries vainly to get in front of her, but Miss Broxton's dander is up, and she is in no mood to brook opposition, especially from a servant. She begins opening doors and peering into rooms. Eventually, after satisfying herself that there is nobody in any of the downstairs rooms, she re-enters the hallway. At which point, something makes her glance up to the first-floor landing. There stands Avice Broxton, wearing a deep-rose silk gown and a sneering expression. She has on a glittering diamond necklace, matching earrings and a couple of sparkling jewelled brooches adorns her ample bust. Her adversary doesn't know it, but this is an attempt to stop Jasper Broxton from laying his hands on her last few treasures and pawning them. To Miss Broxton, in her hysterical state however, it appears that her hated enemy is flaunting her wealth to further goad her.

"I fail to see what you hope to achieve by bursting into my house in this rude fashion, Clara," Avice Broxton says coldly, taking a few steps downstairs, but remaining at a height whereby she can look down upon Clara Broxton, who clenches her fists compulsively as she glares up at her.

"You know very well why I am here," she exclaims. "You set your servant to spy on us ~ I know all about her letters to you. I believe it was you who placed that scurrilous story in the newspaper. Deny it if you can!"

Avice smiles in a supercilious manner. "I reject your use of the word 'spy'. There is no law against one person writing to another, I believe. And as for your other accusation, my husband is in the same club as various owners of several newspapers, some of whom have written pieces about my family and our business dealings in the past. You come here making wild accusations? Prove it. If you can."

"Where is Ruth? What have you done with her?" Clara Broxton exclaims.

Avice stares at her in complete bewilderment. "What on earth are you talking about? Ruth? I have never set eyes on the wretched girl. Why would I?"

"She has been taken from our house!" Miss Broxton shouts. "Four days ago. Either by you or by Cousin Jasper."

"This is complete nonsense. I know nothing about this," Avice stutters. "You must be mad to accuse me of taking her. And my husband? What on earth are you saying? Are you completely out of your mind?"

"You are lying! I see it in your face!" Clara Broxton cries. "You want to ruin me and my poor sister! You are a vile woman, motivated by greed and envy! But you shall not succeed. Even if we have to spend every penny on lawyers' fees, we will fight you in the courts. We will preserve our good name and reputation, whatever it costs, and we will drag your name down into the dust where it belongs!" and shaking her gloved fist at Avice, she elbows her way past the gathered group of fascinated house servants and barrels through the front door, slamming it shut behind her.

In the silence that follows her departure, the only sound is the ticking of the hall clock. The servants stand frozen, open-mouthed, staring up at their mistress, upon whose face the shock of the violent encounter is slowly being replaced by the dawn of realisation. She descends the stairs. Slowly. Once at the bottom, she reaches for her outdoor mantle and her bonnet. "Tell Peters to bring the carriage round at once," she orders. "The girl has gone! She has gone! I must go and tell my husband the good news at once."

****

As Avice Broxton departs for her husband's place of business, Jack Cully, accompanied by a young detective constable who is learning the ropes, arrives there, and is shown into Broxton's office by his clerk. Broxton, who is in the midst of fending off creditors with more unlikely written promises, greets the two men with an expression of relief.

"Gentlemen ~ you are welcome. I presume you have come to give me news of the whereabouts of those thieves Ackroyd and Guskett? You've tracked them down at last! I congratulate you. Did you get your hands on my money?"

Cully shakes his head. "Alas, that is not why we have come to see you, sir. We are here on quite another matter altogether."

Broxton shifts uneasily in his seat. "Oh yes? Another matter? I am intrigued. Please sit, officers. I am sure I can spare you a few minutes of my valuable time. Though I am a very busy man, as I'm sure you both appreciate."

"I'm sure we both do," Cully says affably. "And we will attempt not to intrude upon your busyness a minute longer than necessary." He gestures towards the young officer. "If you don't mind, my constable will record our conversation in his notebook ~ for training purposes."

Broxton frowns, deliberately glances at his pocket watch. The temperature in the room drops a few degrees. "As I said, I am rather busy …"

"Then allow me to come straight to the point. We are here because we have received information that your niece, Miss Ruth Broxton has recently gone missing. The informant has indicated that either you, or your wife, might be able to throw some light upon her disappearance. I refer you to the article that appeared in *The Inquirer* in which you were quoted as saying she was a fake, only there to secure the family inheritance against your own legitimate claim. Clearly this matters on several criminal levels: impersonation, possible libel, putative kidnapping." Cully smiles blandly. "We await your response, Mr Broxton." He turns to the constable, "Pencil ready, young Sam?"

A short while later, Cully and his protégé quit Broxton's office. The interview, conducted in stilted and muted outrage, has managed to convince Cully that the rather unpleasant businessman did not, in fact, have anything to do with the disappearance of the girl. He shares his thoughts with the young detective constable as they make their way back to Scotland Yard.

"Always watch the hands, young Sam," he says. "A man might be able to control his expression, even his voice, but his hands give him away. If he's lying, you'll see his fingers curling into his palms. The angrier he gets, the tighter they curl. I have known murderers draw blood from the palms of their hands. And my other tip: the more complicated the tale, the more his fingers will twist, interlock and curl together. Now, what did you observe about our man back there?"

Sam pauses, because when you are being trained by an expert like Cully, whose reputation precedes him down every corridor, you must concentrate hard, and thinking and proceeding are not compatible in such a situation.

"His hands didn't do any of those things?" he says.

"Well done, Sam. So what do you deduce?"

"He didn't kidnap the girl?"

"Exactly. In fact, I'd go a step further. The news came as a complete surprise to him. Did you notice how his shoulders and jaw suddenly went rigid when I told him? And he blinked several times. It was clear to me that it was the first time he'd heard of it. The interesting thing will be what he does with the information now."

What Jasper Broxton does with the information is to thrust aside all the polite begging letters he has been composing, and to pen a hasty missive to his lawyer, informing him of this new development and urging him to press home to his cousins that with no heiress, he and his family are now once more the legal inheritors of the Broxton land, properties and monies etc. etc. upon the death of his cousin Margaret. This letter is given straight to his clerk, with instructions to deliver it by hand at once and to wait for a reply.

Scarcely has the clerk departed in haste, than Avice Broxton arrives in a carriage. Almost falling out of it, she rushes into the building, quivering with excitement, the dyed ostrich feathers in her bonnet blowing a gale as she hurries up the stairs.

"I bring news!" she cries, bursting straight into her husband's office. "I bring great news!"

"Oh, I know it already," Jasper Broxton says cooly. He is rearranging the desk furniture while he awaits the return of his clerk. "I have just written to the lawyer. As we know, Margaret cannot possibly last much longer, and I believe this event will finally push her over the edge. Whatever the reason the girl absconded, it is unlikely, in my considered opinion, that she will ever return. We have sown the seed that she is a fake. Whoever has taken her will think twice before contacting my cousins. Even if it was her decision to leave, she will hardly dare to return ~ should she choose to do so, public opprobrium would fall heavily upon her. People do not like a swindler," says the man who, in years of dodgy business dealings, has swindled many, many investors out of thousands of pounds.

Avice places a gloved hand dramatically upon her breast. "My children! How they will rejoice when they hear the news! How their poor lives will be made richer ~ I mean better."

Jasper regards her sourly. "I hope you will contain your enthusiasm for the present," he says. "Margaret yet lives, as far as we know. And there will be ... many expenses incurred in the proving of her Will when she dies. For now, I suggest we do not mention anything. To anybody."

"But ..."

"LISTEN to me, would you!" Jasper raises his voice. "For once in your life, do as you are told. We say nothing. We do nothing. We wait. Now, if this is all you came to tell me, I have business to enact. A roof still has to be kept over our heads, and food put on our table. Which reminds me: I shall not be home for supper tonight."

Avice's lower lip protrudes. She glares at her husband, but his head is now bent over his papers and he is fussing with them and deliberately ignoring her. Silently fuming, she returns to the carriage and orders the driver to take her to one of the big department stores in Oxford Street where her husband has an account. She has been forbidden to spend any more money there, but in the light of current events, she is going to ignore that. After all, if her husband can wine and dine his latest lady friend, she can treat herself to some new gloves and a nice tea. At the very least.

****

Miss Clara Broxton returns to the house she shares with her younger sister Margaret. By the time she has reached her street, her temper has cooled somewhat, and she is even beginning to feel a slight sense of shame. She was not brought up to express her feelings, to shout and accuse people. In her mind's eye, she sees the stern figure of nanny, starched apron, and cap, shaking a disapproving finger at her and saying sternly: 'That's *quite* enough of that, Miss Clara. I think it's straight off to bed at once and NO supper!'

Turning the corner, her eye is caught and transfixed by a small crowd gathered outside the house. Miss Broxton picks up the pace and approaches the crowd close enough to hear what is being said. What she hears is enough to drive her through them and up the front steps. For the second time that day Clara Broxton hurtles at unladylike speed into another house, this time her own, crying out: "Margaret? My dear sister ~ I am here!"

Too late. Ah, far, far too late to stroke that pale sisterly brow, to whisper words of comfort, to hold a limp hand in hers and beg forgiveness for every cross word, every unkind thought. The body of Margaret Broxton lies on her bed, hands folded on her breast, eyes closed. The blinds are down, the curtains drawn. Candles have been lit, and in the soft light, her face looks remarkably peaceful for someone who has spent most of her short life a semi-invalid, and the last few seconds of it falling headlong down a flight of stairs.

At the sight of her sister, Clara Broxton sinks to the floor, burying her face in her hands. Myriad memories flash upon her inner eye: Margaret's dark eyes shining across the nursery table above a bowl of bread and milk. Watching her sister dancing in the apple orchard, her white sprigged frock whirling about her. The silhouette of her sister standing against a sunlit window, her body curved in the shape of pregnancy. The handywoman holding up a tiny child covered in blood and announcing: 'It's a li'l girl.'

For a long time, she remains crouched on the floor, almost as still as the figure upon the bed. Then, uttering a deep sigh, Clara Broxton rises, briefly places a hand upon the dead woman's brow, and quits the chamber. There are matters of an official nature that must now be enacted. She wipes her eyes, squares her shoulders, and descends the stairs. She has work to do. The show must go on.

****

And so to the funeral of Miss Margaret Broxton, which is carried out with all the pomp and ritual that such an event demands. After ordering the mirrors in every room to be covered, and a bow of black crepe to be tied to the front doorknob to indicate that a death had taken place within, Clara Broxton betakes herself to the West End, where she visits Jay's retail establishment. There, she orders for herself a couple of fine silk dresses, black for the first six months of her mourning period, then several dresses in grey and mauve for when she will go into half-mourning. All are of the highest quality and hand made. For the rest of the household, she buys cheaper bombazine dresses, off the peg.

It seems that no expense is going to be spared to give Margaret Broxton the finest society funeral, despite her absence from it for most of her life. Locks of the dead woman's hair are snipped and made into various mourning brooches and a ring, which Clara declares that she will never take off her finger until the day she too casts off this mortal coil and goes to be with her beloved sister in Paradise.

The death notice and the arrangements for the funeral are reported in all the better social journals, satiating those readers whose nerves have been jangled during the 'pandemic', and now require something new to occupy their emotional bandwidth. They take an unprecedented interest in every detail, much to the anger and chagrin of Jasper Broxton, who can only fume in silence as he watches his cousin fritter away what he considers to be 'his' money on a fine carriage drawn by six black-plumed horses, a set of official mutes, and the acquisition of a plot in Highgate Cemetery, complete with statue of weeping marble angel (to be erected post burial).

"She's doing it on purpose," he snarls, as he throws down a copy of *The London Illustrated Journal* onto the dining table. "She knows we can't stop her spending money on a funeral. Damn her. Once the Will is proved, she won't get a penny from me. Let her starve in a garret for all I care."

Johanna Broxton, who has been noisily slurping turtle soup, sets down her spoon with a small sputter, showering the white damask tablecloth with stains. "Do I *have* to go to the funeral?" she inquires, pulling a face.

"We are members of the family, so of course we must all go," her mother says tartly. "Shedleigh will come home for it. Luckily, he has a dark suit, so we won't be put to any extra expense. As for you ~ you are not expected to go into mourning, so I will get someone to iron your white frock. That will do."

"But I can't get into my white frock any longer," Johanna grumbles. "It is much too tight and too short."

Avice glares at her daughter. "Please do not create problems, Johanna. It is a difficult time for your Papa and I. I will ask one of the maids to let out the seams and the hem. Nobody will be looking at you, in any case. And don't pull that face. Remember: your dear Papa is about to inherit all of the Broxton fortune. Soon, there will be big changes for us. Perhaps we will be moving to a house in Mayfair or Knightsbridge, with a decent cook and proper ladies' maid for me at last, who knows. So a little sacrifice at this moment is not too much to ask or expect, is it?" She steals a sly glance across the table at her husband.

Jasper Broxton clamps his lips tightly. He has no intention of pandering to Avice's many expense-incurring fantasies. Once his creditors have been paid off, and after laying aside monies for Shedleigh's future, and a smaller sum as a dowry for Johanna, he intends to liquidate as much of the Broxton assets as he reasonably can and put the money into new and profitable investments. Some concessions may be made to his greedy wife. But not nearly as much as she hopes for. After all, it is his inheritance. And he has waited long enough to get his hands on it.

The day of Margaret Broxton's funeral dawns, cloudy, with a spattering of rain. The sky is the colour of dirty ointment. The carriages arrive in front of the house mid-morning and the coffin is carried out. It is followed by Miss Clara Broxton in a black costume, a bonnet and heavy veil. She is supported by one of the maids. The crowd that has assembled, because there is no spectacle so enjoyable as a posh society funeral, removes its caps as a mark of respect, as the carriages clop slowly along the towards the parish church of All Saints, that neither lady attended.

Just as the service commences, Jack Cully slips quietly and unobtrusively into a gallery pew, thus giving him oversight of the attendees. He spies Miss Landseer, who is there by invitation, and members of the Broxton family, sitting on the opposite side to Miss Clara and barely containing their indifference to the service.

As the last mournful hymn is sung, Cully leaves the church and moves to the shade of a cypress tree, where he can get a good look at the onlookers who have gathered to see the coffin and the cortège leave. It is possible, even at this late date, that the orphan Ruth might be tempted out from wherever she has been hiding. Or the blackmailers put in an appearance. But the erstwhile Broxton heiress does not show, even though it is impossible, unless she is living in a cellar, not to know that if ever there was a right time to reveal herself, it is now.

Cully therefore concludes, on the balance of probability, that Lucy Landseer was right: Ruth is not the late Margaret Broxton's abandoned offspring after all, and further, that the true heiress, whoever she is and wherever she is, will never now be discovered.

****

So what actually has happened to the orphan Ruth? And where is she? To answer that, we must return to the fateful meeting between Avice Broxton and Sarah the housemaid. On her return, Sarah allows her temper to cool, biding her time, while working out the finer details of her plan. Then two days later, she enters Ruth's bedroom in the early morning with a jug of hot water, as usual. The girl is still asleep. Ruth pours the water into a china basin before going over to the bed and shaking Ruth sharply by the shoulder.

"Wake up now, Ruth," she says. "And sit up. I want to talk to you."

The girl opens her eyes. "Morning, Sarah," she says sleepily.

"Morning. Sit. Up. Now!"

Ruth sits bolt upright, eyes wide.

"Now, listen, very carefully," Sarah says, seating herself on the edge of the bed. "You aren't happy here, are you? Don't deny it ~ I have eyes in my head. And you know deep down, and we all know too, that Miss Margaret ain't your real mother. You look nuffing like each other. So, here's a suggestion: how would you like to come on a little adventure with me?"

"Where are we going?" the girl asks, intrigued.

"Somewhere a long way from here," Sarah answers. "How'd you like to go on a nice big steam train up to Scotland?"

"With you?"

Sarah nods.

"And would I be coming back here?"

"Do you want to?"

The girl pulls a face. "I thought it'd be different. But it isn't. I can't do anything right, can I? It's like being back in the orphanage 'cept I don't do any scrubbing and I ain't ~ I *haven't* got any friends. And now you tell me Mama isn't my Mama. So maybe I'll come with you."

"Good girl," Sarah says, smiling encouragingly. "Now, this is what we're going to do: on Saturday, the doctor's coming to look at Miss Margaret. While he's busy, and Miss Clara is in the bedroom with them, you'll sneak out of the house. Take whatever clothes and things you want. I'll stand guard to make sure you ain't seen. Here's the address of a friend: she'll put you up. Wait until I come for you. It won't be long. Then we'll be off on the train to Edinburgh."

"What will we do when we get there?"

"I'm going to open a nice little boarding house. Always wanted to be my own boss. And you can be my helper. How do you fancy that?"

The girl is silent for a few minutes. "Will they be cross?"

Sarah shrugs. "Don't know. Don't care. I've been a servant since I was your age. It's time I struck out on my own. As for you ~ their cousin knows you ain't the real heiress, and he's going to make a mort of trouble for the sisters very soon. Lawyers. Maybe police. Best to leave before it happens. You don't want to end up in prison, do you?"

Ruth shakes her head vigorously. She hugs her thin knees with her hands. "But won't it cost a lot of money?"

Sarah the spy smiles a cat-in-a-creamshop smile. "Don't you worry about that, my girl. I got it all under control."

And so, the following Saturday, Ruth packs her clothes, a scrapbook, and a few trinkets in a blanket, as she was bid, and under Sarah's watchful eye, leaves the Broxton establishment. And the next day, while the house is in an uproar over her absence, Sarah quietly slips into Margaret Broxton's bedroom and helps herself to the contents of her mistress' jewel case, on the basis that she never wears any of it, so it is fine to take whatever she wants, and after packing her traps and selling a couple of the rings, she meets up with Ruth at her temporary lodgings.

Next morning, the two catch the Flying Scotsman from Kings Cross, and by early evening they have reached Waverly Station, where, under a sky pierced by white stars, Mrs Susan Brown and her niece Rose hand their tickets to the ticket porter, pass through the barrier and vanish into the city. And that is the last we or anybody else will ever hear of them.

****

It is now two weeks since the body of Margaret Broxton has been laid to rest, and so it is therefore time for her Will to be read. Miss Broxton arrives promptly at the office of the family solicitor, Mr Darius Shrubsole, and is shown politely and discreetly into his inner sanctum. Shrubsole was once a young eager solicitor in the time of her parents and is now an ancient individual who has seen out her parents and looks likely to see out the rest of the family. His voice may be quavery, his hands gnarled and swollen with arthritis, but his eye is keen, and his brain is as sharp as a sharpened nail and as he sits her down and fusses over his documents, she feels a sense of relief that he is 'about her business'.

Even though she occupied so little space in the house they shared for many years, the absence of her sister is a source of pain. Clara Broxton keeps butting up against it, like a bruise. The social rituals around bereavement means that she has not left the house since Margaret was buried. She has passed the time reducing the staff and responding to the sympathy cards ~ many from people she scarcely knows, and registering with various teaching agencies. It has been several years since she was employed full-time in her chosen profession ~ her sister's declining health forbade taking up a permanent post. She suspects that she may have to strike out on her own now. It is unlikely that her cousin will allow her any money to live on once he gets his hands on the Broxton inheritance.

The door opens and Jasper Broxton and his wife enter the room. Both are still wearing deepest mourning, as befits the occasion, but the appearance of grief is slightly offset by the expressions of triumph on their faces. After giving them a few seconds to settle, and offer their insincere sympathies, Mr Shrubsole, solicitor, clears his throat and opens the folder containing the last Will and Testament of Miss Margaret Broxton, spinster. He begins to read.

The silence that follows the reading of the short Will is so tangible it could almost be cut up and served in slices. Nobody moves. Except for the solicitor, who returns the document calmly to its manila folder. He looks up. "I think that is all I have to impart," he says. "The wishes of the deceased are very clear … hmm … all properties, investments, dividends, monies and personal items are to go to the eldest female child of Miss Margaret Broxton."

"But … but … there IS no child!" Jasper Broxton exclaims, his fingers practically shredding the brim of his beaver top hat. "There never was a child: it was all a hoax."

The lawyer studies his angry face in a detached manner. "The wording of the Will clearly states, 'the eldest female child'. It does not specify an actual named child, merely a child in the abstract. As I recall from my exchange of correspondence with the deceased, admittedly a while ago, she was very adamant that such a child existed, and that therefore she, the aforementioned child, despite the circumstances pertaining to her birth, was the legal and legitimate heir to the Broxton estates, *et cetera*. Whether she ever believed that the child that was living in her house at the time of her demise was, or was not, the actual child mentioned in her Will, was not a conversation she ever initiated with me, nor did I presume to question her upon the matter. I was merely given my instructions, which I have carried out exactly as she requested."

"But …" Jasper splutters, "the monies ~ where will the rents and income from the farm and the other properties go?"

The lawyer regards him evenly. "All monies and other income will be kept in trust against the appearance of the eldest daughter of the late Miss Margaret Broxton."

"So we will get NOTHING? NOTHING?? How DARE she!" Jasper Broxton has now gone bright red in the face. "How dare she do this! We will contest it! I will go straight to my lawyer. Oh yes ~ do not think I have any intention of letting it lie!" He turns to Clara Broxton, "You knew about this, didn't you? You were in on the swindle!"

She bridles. "I know nothing. I was not privy to my sister's correspondence, nor her final wishes. You may believe me or not believe me. It makes little difference and I do not care either way." She addresses the lawyer. "Thank you, Mr Shrubsole. I will make my immediate preparations on the basis of my sister's final wishes. For now, I bid you good day."

Miss Clara Broxton rises and walks briskly out of the room without looking at, or acknowledging her cousin and his thunderstruck wife, who both instantly leap to their feet.

"Stop ~ Clara, stop!" Jasper commands, hurrying after her. "You cannot leave. I have not finished with you!"

Mr Shrubsole waits. There is the sound of a brief kerfuffle in the outer office, then the door is closed. Ah well. Wills. There you are. He turns back to his documents.

****

A few hours earlier, before the explosive meeting with the Broxton lawyer takes place, Violet Cully is waiting patiently outside the school gate for her friend May Higgins to arrive. Sometimes she is late ~ her rides are now reliant upon any free cabby picking her up. But Violet always waits for her. If May is to receive a late mark, she will share it.

Smart carriages arrive, disgorge girls, and depart. The pavements are full of female students, laughing, teasing each other, swinging their schoolbags as they climb the steps and enter the building. Still Violet waits. Eventually, a hansom cab draws up outside the gate. It is brand new, the brass fittings gleaming, the paintwork immaculate. The cab is pulled by a black horse, its coat so shiny you can almost see your reflection, its hooves oiled and polished. The horse has a white star on its forehead, and its mane and tail are plaited with red ribbons. On the box sit May's father, a red ribbon tied round his whip handle.

Violet claps her hands in delight, as the cab door opens and May scrambles out. Her father touches his hat to them both with the end of the whip, as he always used to do, then lightly flicks it across the horse's back. The cab pulls smartly away.

"What has happened?" Violet asks. "Who is the horse?"

May tucks her hand through her friend's arm. "The horse is called Diamond," she tells her as the two make their way into the school. "I named him, because of the di'mond on his forehead."

"And the cab?"

"A gift! Pa has his regulars, people he drives to the City every day and then takes them back home in the evening. Some of them are rich men, and when they heard of our misfortune, they all got together and raised a collection for a new cab and a horse. Can you believe it?"

"I wouldn't believe it except I've seen it with my own eyes," Violet says. "I am so pleased for you."

They join the throng of chattering girls hurrying to their various classrooms, passing, as they do so, Johanna Broxton and her small crowd of devotees (even the worst bully has some). But this time, the small crowd has been augmented by a bigger crowd. In the middle, Johanna, seated on a window ledge (which is strictly against the school rules), is regaling her rapt audience with lavish descriptions of the new house, her new clothes and all the treats awaiting her, once her father becomes heir to the vast Broxton fortune.

The two girls walk past, deliberately averting their gaze.

"She is going to be quite insufferable from now on, isn't she?" May mutters.

Violet rolls her eyes. "I fear so. Never mind, we shall just have to avoid her. With a bit of luck, she'll decide we are far too poor and lowly to pay us any attention, as she is so rich. Though probably not. She won't change. My mother always says all the money in the world can't buy you happiness ~ although," she adds as they find their desks, "it can buy you a brand-new cab and a new horse!"

*****

After leaving the solicitor's office, and then conducting a furious one-sided conversation with his cousin, which is witnessed by several delighted passers-by, Jasper and Avice Broxton part company. They do not exchange a single word: the one because he is too incandescent with fury to speak civilly to the wife of his bosom, the other because she is thinking guiltily of all the dresses she has ordered, the new china for the dining room, and the bonnets and shawls and wondering how she will conceal their purchase now that the promised money is not going to be pouring into their bank account.

Meanwhile Clara Broxton, much shaken by the contents of her sister's Will and the behaviour of her cousin, betakes herself to a small tea-room. Over a pot of Indian tea and a small piece of cake, she reviews her options. She has some savings ~ enough to tide her over for the next few months while she seeks employment. Even so, she has spent lavishly on her sister's funeral, and there are bills to be paid.

As she stirs sugar into her tea, she thinks about the girl Ruth. Perhaps she was too strict with her. Not understanding enough. Was it her regime of daily lessons and constant chipping away at the girl's manners and deportment that drove her away? If she had the time again, she would act very differently, she decides.

But maybe there is a possibility of turning the clock back. She recalls the scurrilous article in *The Inquirer* ~ clearly the work of her unscrupulous cousin. But might there now be other articles? Ones that could be read by Ruth, or those looking after her ~ articles that would tempt her into returning to her true family sphere? If this happened, if the girl could somehow be coaxed back, then she, Clara, could remain in the London house. And pay her bills. And live comfortably for the rest of her life. She finishes her tea and sets off determinedly in the direction of Fleet Street.

****

Next morning, readers of *The London Illustrated Gazette* are treated to a heart-rending article about an abandoned female baby (the circumstances are left deliberately vague, but the suggestion is that it was not the fault of the mother), its only link to its true family a shawl and a jewelled locket. The piece does not go unnoticed by the inhabitants of Regent's Terrace, where the *paterfamilias* reads it and immediately vows to get even with his cousin.

The following day, readers of *The Inquirer* are presented with an article written in the purple prose of Richard Dandy, decrying those people in society who choose to abandon their offspring, forcing hardworking members of the public to pay for their upbringing through their taxes. By Thursday, *The Gazette's* story incorporates hints of an unnamed wicked uncle who might have plotted to get rid of the child by some nefarious means. By Friday, *The Inquirer* retaliates with a stinging indictment upon those who suddenly 'rediscover' their abandoned offspring years later, when they sniff out the scent of an inheritance.

And so, while behind the scenes the Broxton lawyers battle on with little sign of any resolution, the general public delights itself reading about the war of attrition between two so-called respectable families, so much so that several London impresarios quietly abandon the idea of putting on their usual Christmas panto, and decide to commission a 'Lost Babe in London' script instead. Possibly incorporating songs and a ballet.

****

Meanwhile, the leaves in London's parks and gardens begin to turn yellow and red, then brown. Birds start singing their Autumn songs. The pale daylight leaks from the sky even earlier than before, and nights begin to draw in. The lamp-lighters start their rounds in the late afternoon, propping their ladders against the lampposts as they ignite each golden globe, and over in Flask Walk, Mrs Lilith Marks places her order for sacks of currants and candied peel, anticipating all the upcoming orders for her famous Christmas cakes.

A misty rain is softly falling as Jack Cully makes his way back home. He has spent another day out of his office interviewing witnesses and underground railway staff about some train robberies in the Farringdon tunnel. There have been a couple of them over the past week, and already a rumour is starting to go around that the underground is not safe for people to travel on.

It has been a busy few days with little pause, and Cully is thinking about how glad he will be to reach his own fireside, and what his wife Emily will have cooked for his supper. He leaves the clatter of the high street, with its small shops, nimbuses of gold, and the sound of a barrel-organ in the distance, and turns the corner into a small street of terraced brick properties.

As he quickens his pace, Jack Cully passes his neighbours' houses, where he spies kettles on hearths, fires in grates, a spread tea-table, a woman pouring tea for her husband, a man mending a pair of boots, and children playing with their toys. All is warmth and colour. With a sigh of relief, glad to get out of the damp and mist, Cully finds his door-key and lets himself into his own house, which smells fragrantly of herrings, and where Emily and his youngest daughter are laying the table ready. In one corner of the small parlour Violet and her friend May have their heads bent over their books ~ they are preparing for a presentation on the Egyptians, an activity that demands much of their after-school time. Today, it is Violet's turn to host.

Emily greets him with a smile of welcome, before returning to the stove to serve the meal. Cully picks up his youngest, sets her on his shoulders and goes to wash the grime of the day from his face and hands. Over the family's supper of herrings and potato, followed by stewed fruit, Violet entertains the company with instructions on how to construct a pyramid, and the various procedures necessary to embalm a Pharoah ~ which earns her a gentle 'not while we are eating, please Vi,' rebuke from her mother.

Cully is about to make a start on washing the pots, when he hears the sound of a horse's hooves and a set of wheels coming down the street and stopping at the door.

"I think your pa is here, May," he calls, to a chorus of disappointment.

Cully goes to open the front door. The two men greet each other politely. They haven't been properly introduced to each other before, though tales of their lives and occupations have been copiously shared by their respective daughters. Now, they shake hands and exchange Christian names.

"I hear you have a new cab, Fred," Cully says.

"Maybe you'd care to step outside and take a look at it, Jack?" May's father says.

Cully is about to respond that as he can see, he, Cully, is in his shirtsleeves and slippers, when he catches the edge of the other's glance, and reads the desperation in it. This is a man with a problem. A problem he wants to share. There is a brief pause. Then,

"Well, now, I think I'd like nothing better. Let me change into my boots and grab my jacket and my tobacco pouch. You'll join me in a smoke, I dare say?"

Outside, the rain has eased off, leaving behind ragged discs of roadside puddles. The damp has settled upon the pavement, where it sends up a greasy sparkle under the pale lamplight. The black horse blows through its nostrils and shakes its head. May's father throws a blanket over its back and speaks a few words, patting its shiny neck.

Cully fills his pipe, then offers the other man his pouch. They smoke in companionable silence for a while. Cully waits, biding his time patiently. Countless interrogations have taught him the value of silence, and stillness. Eventually, May's father reaches into his coat pocket and brings out a crumpled copy of *The Gazette*.

"I'm not much of a reading man," he says. "Don't have the time, what with the cabbing and taking care of the horse. The wife's the big reader in the family ~ and young May, of course. But a fare left this in my cab, or I'd not have seen it." He folds the newspaper back to the article on Margaret Broxton and shows it to Cully.

"Now, I'm going to tell you a story, Jack. And when I've done, I'd like your true opinion about it." He takes a few more puffs of his pipe. "It happened some years ago. I'd just started in the cabbing business ~ I was driving for someone else in those days. I'd married the wife, and we was very happy together, despite her being a foreigner and not quite used to our ways yet. We'd rented a nice little two room cottage. Only one thing was missing: we didn't have a child. Not a living one ~ twice, we'd hoped, but each time, she lost it.

"So, that evening, I was waiting at the cab rank when up comes this woman. She was all veiled and carrying something wrapped in a shawl. When she asked me to drive her to a certain orphanage, I guessed what was in the bundle she was carrying. Anyway, I drove her to where she wanted to go, then I set her down and drove a little further down the street and stopped the cab. I waited a bit, then got down and walked back. Sure enough, there was the bundle on the steps of the orphanage. The woman was nowhere to be seen. She'd left the baby and run off. I think you can guess the rest."

"You took the baby home and brought her up as your own?"

"That's it exactly. In the shawl, we found a locket. I kept it and the shawl; it seemed like the right thing to do. We called her May because that was the month when I found her. And now I read in this newspaper that she is really the daughter of some rich woman, and she has an inheritance and the family want her back." May's father turns his head away. "It is breaking my heart, Jack. I haven't slept properly for nights. It is just worrying away inside me, and I don't know what to do for the best."

Jack Cully lets a few seconds pass. Then he says, quietly, "She is your daughter, Fred. Not theirs. No doubt in my mind whatsoever about that. You took her in when they didn't want her. You gave her a name. She is far more yours than she ever was theirs. Now, maybe I am wrong, but it always seems to me that the best thing a child can have is a nice home, food on the table and parents who love them. All the money in the world doesn't buy you a single one of those. Never can, never will. Besides, the woman who gave birth to her is dead. The sister, who was happy to leave her on a doorstep all those years ago, remember, without a backward glance, will never love her like you both do."

The cabby sighs gustily. "Jack, it's a real facer and no mistake. Say, for instance, I did come forward, and showed this sister the shawl and the locket, and May got to live with her and be brought up a proper lady, do you think she'd let her visit us, every now and then?"

Cully puts a firm hand on his companion's shoulder. "If you choose to do that, I believe you will never see your daughter again. But it is up to you, Fred. You have to decide what is the right thing to do."

They stand in silence for a while. Then Cully turns and goes back into the house, followed a few seconds later by May's father.

"You were a long time out there, Pa," Violet remarks, as May packs up her schoolbag ready to leave.

"Well, there's a lot to see with a new cab and a new horse," Cully replies.

Later that evening, when the streets are quiet and deserted, a lone hansom cab approaches the right-hand Canal Bridge, near the cross-path to Chalk Farm. The cab halts and the driver steps down off the box. He walks onto the bridge, leans over the parapet and drops a small bundle into the water below. Then he gets back onto the box, flicks his whip and the cab rattles away.

****

Time passes. And here is Felix Lawrence, former general surgeon at the London Hospital, dismounting from an omnibus outside Fenchurch Station. He wears a dark suit, black gloves and a black hatband, for having recently buried his mother, he now has no reason to remain in England. Nor does he intend to. He carries a travelling bag, his main luggage having gone ahead of him. From the station, he catches a train to Gravesend where, after an overnight stay at the King's Head (a comfortable bed, but rather a poor breakfast), he is booked on the Imperial Castle, a foreign steamer bound for Indochina.

Lawrence will serve as physician aboard various ships for the next twenty years. During this time, he will encounter a shy, reserved Swiss-French physician called Alexandre Yersin, an affiliate of the Pasteur Institute, and will share with him his thoughts, observations and plague notes from his time in

England. In 1892, Yersin, relocated to China, will discover the cause and cycle of transmission of the plague bacillus, leading to the production of the first effective treatments.

****

Just as one man is preparing to leave his former place of employment, another is about to re-enter his. Ex-Detective Inspector Stride approaches Scotland Yard, carrying a mug of steaming treacly coffee in one hand. In the background, a newsboy shouts the latest headlines: the crash of Broxton Business Investment & Financial Services with the arrest of its founder for swindling investors out of thousands of pounds, but his cries barely register as Stride pushes through the entrance door to Scotland Yard, greeting the desk-duty constable cheerily as he does so.

Stride is thoroughly enjoying his retirement. Over the past few months, he has involved himself in two major inquiries without a single piece of paperwork crossing his desk. He has made inroads into his memoirs (current title: *The Adventures of a Scotland Yard Detective*). He has avoided various tiresome domestic duties. His heart is light, as he carries his mug down to the basement, where the day's research awaits him.

There are those who say you can't recapture the past, but they are wrong. Here it is: shelves of box files and tin trunks containing the thefts, murders and strange and uncanny events that have taken place in London from the foundation of the police force by Sir Robert Peel, to the day that young Constable Stride took his first tentative steps onto the cobbled streets of the great city, to the day that he metaphorically hung up his boots.

With a sigh of contentment, ex-Detective Inspector Leo Stride pulls out a chair and contemplates the task ahead of him, and a set of newly-sharpened pencils. All reported crimes and misdemeanours are here. And he has all the time in the world to revisit them. But first, he has an important addition. Taking up a fresh sheet of paper, Stride heads it: *The Strange Case of the Plague that Never Happened*, and begins writing.

Finis

Thank you for reading this book. If you have enjoyed it, why not leave a review on Amazon, a comment on social media, or recommend it to other readers? All reviews, however long or short, help me to continue doing what I do.

Printed in Great Britain
by Amazon